LANCELOT OF THE LAIK

ANONYMOUS

MYTHBANK

Arthurian Legends

www.arthurlegends.com

MythBank

www.mythbank.com

Cover design by Jason Hamilton.

CONTENTS

ABOUT MYTHBANK

MythBank is a website devoted to the documentation and study of storytelling. As part of that initiative, this collection was created with the purpose of ensuring all public domain classics had attractive, uniform, and readily-available print copies and ebooks.

Through print on demand, many classics that are lesser known or have limited runs can still be available for anyone who wants it, keeping the price steady and reducing the need to search the dregs of used books for a copy that might cost ten times what it's worth.

This and other classics are all available as free ebooks in multiple formats on MythBank.com, where you will also find podcasts and audiobooks on some of your favorite classics. Check out Great Books Daily for a daily dose of public domain audiobooks.

We hope you enjoy this collection of classics, and recommend you visit our website to learn more. Additionally, you will find other classics in this collection that are designed to match the same branding and tone of this volume, so they look amazing on your shelf or your device. Check them out!

BOOK 1

The soft morow ande the lustee Aperill,
The wynter set, the stormys in exill,
Quhen that the brycht and fresch illumynare
Uprisith arly in his fyré chare
His hot courss into the orient,
And frome his spere his goldine stremis sent
Wpone the grond, in maner off mesag
One every thing, to ualkyne thar curage,
That natur haith set wnder hire mycht,
Boith gyrss and flour and every lusty uicht,
And namly thame that felith the assay
Of lufe, to schew the kalendis of May,
Throw birdis songe with opine vox one hy
That sessit not one lufaris for to cry,
Lest thai forghet, throw slewth of ignorans,
The old wsage of Lovis observans.
And fromme I can the bricht face asspy,
It deuit me no langare fore to ly,
Nore that love schuld sleuth into me finde,
Bot walkine furth, bewalinge in my mynde

The dredful lyve endurit al to longe,
Sufferans in love of sorouful harmys stronge,
The scharpe dais and the hevy yerys
Quhill Phebus thris haith passith al his speris,
Uithoutine hope ore traistinge of comfort.
So be such meine fatit was my sort.
Thus in my saull rolinge al my wo,
My carful hart carving cann in two
The derdful suerd of lovis hot dissire;
So be the morow set I was afyre
In felinge of the access hot and colde,
That haith my hart in sich a fevir holde;
Only to me thare was nonne uthir ess
Bot thinkine qhow I schulde my lady pless.
The scharp assay and ek the inwart peine
Of dowblit wo me neulyngis cann constrein
Quhen that I have remembrit one my thocht
How sche, quhois bewté al my harmm haith wrocht,
Ne knouith not how I ame wo-begonne,
Nor how that I ame of hire servandis onne.
And in myself I cann nocht fynde the meyne
Into quhat wyss I sal my wo compleine.
Thus in the feild I walkith to and froo,
As thochtful wicht that felt of nocht bot woo,
Syne to o gardinge, that wess weil besenn
Of quiche the feild was al depaynt with grenn.
The tendyre and the lusty flouris new
Up throue the grenn upone thar stalkis grew
Aghane the sone, and thare levis spred,
Quharwith that al the gardinge was iclede.
That Pryapus, into his tyme before,
In o lustear walkith nevir more.
And al about enveronyt and iclosit

One sich o wyss, that none within supposit
Fore to be senn with ony uicht thareowt.
So dide the levis clos it all about.
Thar was the flour, thar was the Quenn Alphest,
Rycht wering being of the nychtis rest,
Wnclosing ganne the crownel for the day;
The brycht sone illumynit haith the spray,
The nychtis sobir ande the most schowris,
As cristoll terys withhong upone the flouris
Haith upwarpith in the lusty aire,
The morow makith soft, ameyne, and faire.
And the byrdis thar mychty voce out-throng
Quhill al the wood resonite of thar songe
That gret confort till ony uicht it wer
That plessith thame of lustenes to here.
Bot gladness til the thochtful, ever mo
The more he seith, the more he haith of wo.
Thar was the garding with the flouris ovrfret,
Quich is in posy fore my lady set,
That hire represent to me oft befor
And thane also; thus al day gan, be sor
Of thocht, my gost with torment occupy,
That I becamme into one exasy,
Ore slep, or how I wot; bot so befell
My wo haith done my livis gost expell,
And in sich wiss weil long I can endwr;
So me betid o wondir aventur.
As I thus lay, rycht to my spreit uas senn
A birde, that was as ony lawrare grenn,
Alicht and sayth into hir birdis chere,
"O woful wrech that levis into were!
To schew the thus the God of Love me sent
That of thi service no thing is content,

For in his court yhoue levith in disspar
And uilfully sustenis al thi care
And schapith no thinge of thine awn remede
Bot clepith ay and cryith apone dede.
Yhow callith the birdis be morow fro thar bouris;
Yhoue devith boith the erbis and the flouris
And clepit hyme unfaithful King of Love.
Yow devith hyme into his rigne abufe;
Yhow tempith hyme, yhoue doith thiself no gud;
Yhoue are o monn of wit al destitude.
Wot yhoue nocht that al livis creatwre
Haith of thi wo into his hand the cwre?
And set yhoue clep one erbis and one treis,
Sche heris not thi wo, nore yhit sche seis;
For none may know the dirkness of thi thocht
Ne blamyth her thi wo sche knowith nocht.
And it is weil accordinge it be so
He suffir harme, that to redress his wo
Previdith not; for long ore he be sonde,
Holl of his leich, that schewith not his uound.
And of Ovid the autor schall yhow knaw,
Of lufe that seith, for to consel or schow,
The last he clepith althir best of two;
And that is suth and sal be ever mo.
And Love also haith chargit me to say
Set yhoue presume, ore beleif, the assay
Of his service, as it wil ryne ore go,
Preswme it not, fore it wil not be so;
Al magré thine a servand schal yow bee.
And as tueching thine adversytee,
Complen and sek of the ramed, the cwre;
Ore, gif yhow likith, furth thi wo endure."
And, as me thocht, I ansuerde againn

Thus to the byrde, in wordis schort and plane:
"It ganyth not, as I have harde recorde,
The servand for to disput with the lord;
Bot well he knowith of al my uo the quhy
And in quhat wyss he hath me set, quhar I
Nore may I not, nore can I not attane,

Nore to hir hienes dare I not complane."
"Ful," quod the bird, "lat be thi nyss dispare,
For in this erith no lady is so fare,
So hie estat, nore of so gret empriss
That in hireself haith uisdome ore gentrice,
Yf that o wicht, that worthy is to be
Of Lovis court schew til hir that he
Servith hire in lovis hartly wyss
That schall tharfor hyme hating or dispiss.
The God of Love thus chargit the, at schort,
That to thi lady yhoue thi wo report.
Yf yhoue may not, thi plant schall yhou urit.
Se, as yhoue cane, be maner oft endit
In metir, quhich that no man haith susspek,
Set ofttyme thai contenyng gret effecc;
Thus one sume wyss yhow schal thi wo dwclar.
And for thir sedulis and thir billis are
So generall and ek so schort at lyte
And swme of thaim is lost the appetit,
Sum trety schall yhoue for thi lady sak,
That wnkouth is, als tak one hand and mak
Of love ore armys or of sum othir thing
That may hir oneto thi remembryng brynge,
Qwich soundith not oneto no hevyness
Bot oneto gladness and to lusteness
That yhoue belevis may thi lady pless,

To have hir thonk and be oneto hir ess
That sche may wit in service yhow art one.
Faire weil," quod sche, "thus schal yhow the dispoe
And mak thiself als mery as yhoue may;
It helpith not thus fore to wex alway."
With that the bird sche haith hir leif tak,
For fere of quich I can onone to wak.
Sche was ago, and to myself thocht I
Quhat may this meyne? Quhat may this signify?
Is it of troucht or of illusioune?
Bot finaly, as in conclusioune,
Be as be may, I schal me not discharge
Sen it apperith be of Lovis charg
And ek myne hart nonne othir bissynes
Haith bot my ladice service, as I gess.
Among al utheris I schal one honde tak
This litil occupatioune for hire sak.
Bot hyme I pray, the mychty Gode of Love,
That sitith hie into his spir abuf
(At command of o wyss quhois visioune
My gost haith takin this opunioune)
That my lawboure may to my lady pless
And do wnto hir ladeschip sum ess
So that my travell be nocht tynt, and I
Quhat utheris say setith nothing by.
For wel I know that be this worldis famme
It schal not be bot hurting to my namme
Quhen that thai here my febil negligens
That empit is and bare of eloquens,
Of discressioune, and ek of retoryk,
The metire and the cuning both elyk
So fere discording frome perfeccioune,
Quhilk I submyt to the correccioune

Of thaim the quhich that is discret and wyss
And enterit is of Love in the service,
Quhich knouyth that no lovare dare withstonde:
Quhat Love hyme chargit he mot tak one honde,
Deith or defamm or ony maner wo.
And at this tyme with me it stant rycht so
As I that dar makine no demande
To quhat I wot it lykith Love commande.
Tueching his chargis, as with al-destitut,
Within my mynd schortly I conclud
For to fulfyll, for ned I mot do so.
Thane in my thocht rolling to and fro
Quhare that I myhct sum wnkouth mater fynde
Quhill at the last it fell into my mynd
Of o story, that I befor had sene,
That boith of love and armys can contenn,
Was of o knycht clepit Lancelot of the Laik,
The sone of Bane was, King of Albanak,
Of quhois fame and worschipful dedis
Clerkis into diverss bukis redis,
Of quhome I thynk her sumthing for to writ
At Lovis charge, and as I cane endit,
Set men tharin sal by experiens
Know my consait and al my negligens.
Bot for that story is so pasing larg,
Oneto my wit it war so gret o charg
For to translait the romans of that knycht.
It passith fare my cunyng and my mycht;
Myne ignorans may it not comprehende.
Quharfor thareone I wil me not depend
How he was borne, nor how his fader deid
And ek his moder, nore how he was denyed
Efter thare deth, presumyng he was ded,

Of al the lond, nore how he fra that stede
In sacret wyss wnwyst away was tak
And nwrist with the Lady of the Lak.
Nor, in his youth, think I not to tell
The aventouris, quhich to hyme befell,
Nor how the Lady of the Laik hyme had
Oneto the court, quhare that he knycht was mad.
None wist his nome nore how that he was tak
By love and was iwondit to the stak
And throuch and throuch persit to the hart
That al his tyme he couth it not astart;
For thare of Love he enterit in service
Of Wanore throuch the beuté and franchis,
Throuch quhois service in armys he has urocht
Mony wonderis, and perellis he has socht.
Nor how he thor, into his young curage
Hath maid avoue and into lovis rage
In the revenging of o wondit knycht
That cumyne was into the court that nycht.
Into his hed a brokin suerd had he
And in his body also mycht men see
The tronsione of o brokine sper that was,
Quhich no man out dedenyt to aras;
Nor how he haith the wapnis out tak
And his avow apone this wis can mak,
That he schuld hyme reveng at his poware
One every knycht that lovith the hurtare
Better thane hyme, the quhich that uas iwond.
Throw quich avoue in armys hath ben founde
The deth of mony wereoure ful wicht;
For, fro tho vow was knowing of the knycht,
Thare was ful mony o pasage in the londe
By men of armys kepit to withstond

This knycht, of quhome thai ben al set afyre
Thaim to reveng in armys of desir.
Nor how that thane incontynent was send
He and Sir Kay togidder to defend
The Lady of Nohalt, nor how that hee
Governit hyme thare, nore in quhat degré.
Nor how the gret pasing vassolag
He eschevit throue the outragouss curag,
In conquiryng of the sorowful castell.
Nor how he passith doune in the cavis fell
And furth the keys of inchantment brocht,
That al distroyt quhich that thare uas urocht.
Nore howe that he reskewit Sir Gawane,
With his nine falouss into presone tane.
Nore mony uthere diverss adventure,
Quhich to report I tak not in my cwre.
Nor mony assemblay that Gawane gart be maid
To wit his name; nor how that he hyme hade
Wnwist and hath the worschip and empriss;
Nor of the knychtis into mony diverss wyss
Throuch his avoue that hath thare dethis found.
Nor of the sufferans that by Lovis wounde
He in his travel sufferith avermore.
Nor in the Quenis presens how tharfor
By Camelot, into that gret revare,
He was ner dround. I wil it not declare
How that he was in lovis hevy thocht
By Dagenet into the court ibrocht;
Nor how the knycht that tyme he cane persew,
Nor of the gyantis by Camelot he slew;
Nor wil I not her tell the maner how
He slew o knycht, by natur of his vow,
Off Melyholt; nore how into that toune

Thar came one hyme o gret confusione
Of pupil and knychtis al enarmyt;
Nor how he thar haith kepit hyme wnharmyt;
Nor of his worschip, nor of his gret prowes,
Nor his defens of armys in the pres;
Nor how the Lady of Melyhalt that sche
Came to the feild and prayth hyme that he
As to o lady to hir his suerd hath yold,
Nor how he was into hir keping hold.
And mony uthir nobil deid also
I wil report quharfor I lat ovrgo.
For quho thaim lykith forto specyfy
Of one of thaim mycht mak o gret story.
Nor thing I not of his hye rennown
My febil wit to makin mensioune.
Bot of the weris that was scharp and strong,
Richt perellouss, and hath enduryt long;
Of Arthur in defending of his lond
Frome Galiot, sone of the fair Gyonde
That brocht of knychtis o pasing confluens
And how Lancelot of Arthuris hol defens
And of the ueris berith the renownn;
And how he be the wais of fortoune
Tuex the two princis makith the accorde
Of al there mortall weris to concorde;
And how that Venus, siting hie abuf,
Reuardith hyme of travell into love
And makith hyme his ladice grace to have,
And thankfully his service can resave:
This is the mater quhich I think to tell.
Bot stil he mot rycht with the lady duell
Quhill tyme cum eft that we schal of hym spek.
This process mot closine benn and stek,

And furth I wil oneto my mater go.
Bot first I pray and I besek also
Oneto the most conpilour to support,
Flour of poyetis, quhois nome I wil report
To me nor to nonn uthir it accordit
Into our rymyng his namm to be recordit;
For sum suld deme it of presumpsioune
And ek our rymyng is al bot derysioune
Quhen that remembrit is his excellens
So hie abuf that stant in reverans.
The fresch enditing of his Laiting toung
Out throuch this world so wid is yroung
Of eloquens and ek of retoryk.
Nor is nor was nore never beith hyme lyk;
This world gladith of his suet poetry.
His saul i blyss conservyt be forthy;
And yf that ony lusty terme I wryt
He haith the thonk therof and this endit.

EXPLICIT PROLOGUS, ET INCIPIT PRIMUS
    LIBER.

BOOK I

Quhen Tytan withe his lusty heit
Twenty dais into the Aryeit
Haith maid his courss and all with diverss hewis
Aparalit haith the feldis and the bewis,
The birdis amyd the erbis and the flouris
And one the branchis makyne gone thar bouris,
And be the morow singing in ther chere
Welcum the lusty sessone of the yere.
Into this tyme the worthi conqueroure

Arthure, wich had of al this worlde the floure
Of chevelry anerding to his crown--
So pasing war his knychtis in renoune--
Was at Carlill; and hapynnit so that hee
Sojornyt well long in that faire cuntree,
Into whilk tyme into the court thai heire
None aventure, for wich the knyghtis weire
Anoit all at the abiding thare.
Forwhy beholding one the sobir ayre
And of the tyme the pasing lustynes
Can so thir knyghtly hartis to encress
That thei Shir Kay oneto the King haith sende
Beseiching hyme he wold vichsaif to wende
To Camelot the cetee, whare that thei
Ware wont to heryng of armys day be day.
The King forsuth, heryng thare entent,
To thare desir, be schort avysment,
Ygrantid haith; and so the king proponit
And for to pas hyme one the morne disponit.
Bot so befell hyme that nycht to meit
An aperans, the wich oneto his spreit
It semyth that of al his hed the hore
Of fallith and maid desolat; wharfore
The King therof was pensyve in his mynd
That al the day he couth no resting fynde
Wich makith hyme his jorneye to delaye.
And so befell apone the thrid day,
The bricht sone pasing in the west
Hath maid his courss and al thing goith to rest.
The Kinge, so as the story can devyss,
He thoght ageine apone the samyne wyss:
His uombe out fallith uith his hoil syde
Apone the ground and liging hyme besid,

Throw wich anon out of his slep he stert,
Abasit and adred into his hart.
The wich be morow oneto the Qwen he told,
And she ageine to hyme haith ansuer yolde.
"To dremys, sir, shuld no man have respek,
For thei ben thingis veyn, of non affek."
"Well," quod the King, "God grant it so befall."
Arly he ross and gert oneto hyme call
O clerk, to whome that al his hevynes
Tweching his drem shewith he express,
Wich ansuer yaf and seith oneto the Kinge:
"Shir, no record lyith to such thing;
Wharfor now, shir, I praye yow tak no kep
Nore traist into the vanyteis of slep.
For thei are thingis that askith no credens
But causith of sum maner influens,
Empriss of thoght, ore superfleuytee,
Or than sum othir casualytee."
"Yit," quod the King, "I sal nocht leif it so."
And furth he chargit mesingeris to go
Throgh al his realm, withouten more demande,
And bad them stratly at thei shulde comande
All the bishopes and makyng no delay
The shuld appere be the tuenty day
At Camelot with al thar hol clergy
That most expert war for to certefye
A mater tueching to his gost be nyght.
The mesag goith furth with the lettres right.

The King eftsone, within a litill space,
His jornay makith haith frome place to place,
Whill that he cam to Camelot.
The clerkis all, as that the chargit were,

Assemblit war and cam to his presens,
Of his desir to uiting the sentens.
To them that war to hyme most speciall
Furth his entent shauyth he al hall;
By whois conseil of the worthiest
He chesith ten, yclepit for the best,
And most expert and wisest was supposit,
To qwhome his drem all hail he haith disclossit--
The houre, the nyght, and al the cercumstans--
Besichyne them that the signifycans
Thei wald hyme shaw, that he mycht resting fynde
Of it, the wich that occupeid his mynde.
And one of them with al ther holl assent
Saith, "Shire, fore to declare our entent
Upone this matere, ye wil ws delay
Fore to avysing oneto the ninth day."
The King therto grantith haith, bot hee
Into o place that strong was and hye,
He closith them whare thei may nowhare get
Unto the day, the wich he to them set.
Than goith the clerkis sadly to avyss
Of this mater, to seing in what wyss
The Kingis drem thei shal best specefy.
And than the maistris of astronomy
The bookis longyne to ther artis set.
Not was the bukis of Arachell forget,
Of Nembrot, of Danghelome, thei two,
Of Moyses, and of Herynes allsoo.
And seking be ther calcolacioune
To fynd the planetis disposicioune,
The wich thei fond ware wonder evill yset
The samyne nyght the King his sweven met.
So ner the point socht thei have the thing, 30

Thei fond it wonder hevy to the King,
Of wich thing thei waryng into were
To shew the King for dreid of his danger.
Of ane accorde thei planly have proponit
No worde to show, and so thei them disponit.
The day is cumyng and he haith fore them sent,
Besichyne them to shewing ther entent.
Than spak thei all and that of an accorde:
"Shir, of this thing we can no thing recorde,
For we can noght fynd intil our sciens
Tweching this mater ony evydens."
"Now," quod the King, "and be the glorius Lorde,
Or we depart ye shall sumthing recorde;
So pas yhe not, nor so it sall not bee."
"Than," quod the clerkis, "grant ws dais three."
The wich he grantid them, and but delay
The term passith; nothing wold the say,
Wharof the King stondith hevy cherith;
And to the clerkis his visag so apperith
That all thei dred them of the Kingis myght.
Than saith o clerk, "Sir, as the thrid nyght
Ye dremyt, so giffis ws delay
The thrid tyme and to the thrid day."
By whilk tyme thei fundyng haith the ende
Of this mater, als far as shal depend
To ther sciens; yit can thei not avyss
To schewing to the King be ony wyss.
The day is cum; the King haith them besocht;
Bot one no wyss thei wald declar ther thoght.
Than was he wroth into hisself and noyt
And maid his vow that thei shal ben distroyt.
His baronis he commandit to gar tak
Fyve of them oneto the fir stak

And uther fyve be to the gibbot tone;
And the furth with the Kingis charg ar gone.
He bad them into secret wyss that thei
Shud do no harm but only them assey.
The clarkis, dredful of the Kingis ire
And saw the perell of deth and of the fyre,
Fyve, as thei can, has grantit to record,
That uther herde and ben of ther accorde.
And al thei ben yled oneto the King
And shew hyme thus as tueching of this thing.
"Shir, sen that we constrenyt ar by myght
To shaw wich that we knaw nothing aricht,
For thing to cum preservith it allan
To Hyme the wich is every thing certann
Excep the thing that til our knawleg Hee
Hath ordynat of certan for to bee.
Therfor, shir King, we your magnificens
Beseich it turne till ws to non offens
Nor hald ws nocht as learis, thoght it fall
Not in this mater, as that we telen shall."
And that the King haith grantit them, and thei
Has chargit one, that one this wiss sall seye.
"Presumyth, shir, that we have fundyne so:
All erdly honore ye nedist most forgo
And them the wich ye most affy intyll
Shal failye yow, magré of ther will;
And thus we have into this matere founde."
The King, qwhois hart was al wyth dred ybownd,
And askit at the clerkis if thei fynde
By there clergy that stant in ony kynde
Of possibilitee fore to reforme
His desteny, that stud in such a forme,
If in the hevyne is preordynat

On such o wiss his honor to translat.
The clerkis saith, "Forsuth, and we have sene
O thing wharof, if we the trouth shal menn,
Is so obscure and dyrk til our clergye
That we wat not what it shal signefye
Wich causith ws we can it not furth say."
"Yis," quod the King, "as lykith yow ye may,
For wers than this can nat be said for me."
Thane saith o maistir, "Than suthly thus finde we:
Thar is nothing sal sucour nor reskew;
Your worldly honore nedis most adew,
But throuch the watrye lyone, and ek fyne,
On throuch the liche and ek the wattir syne,
And throuch the conseill of the flour; God wot
What this shude menn, for mor ther-of we not."
No word the King ansuerid ayane,
For al this resone thinkith bot in veyne.
He shawith outwart his contenans
As he therof takith no grevans;
But al the nyght it passid nat his thoght.
The dais courss with ful desir he socht,
And furth he goith to bring his mynd in rest
With mony o knyght unto the gret forest.
The rachis gon wncopelit for the deire
That in the wodis makith nois and cheir;
The knychtis with the grewhundis in aweit
Secith boith the planis and the streit.
Doune goith the hart, doune goith the hynd also.
. . . .
The swift grewhund, hardy of assay;
Befor ther hedis nothing goith away.
The King of hunting takith haith his sport
And to his palace home he can resort

Ayan the noon. And as that he was set
Uith all his noble knyghtis at the met,
So cam therin an agit knyght; and hee
Of gret esstat semyt for to bee,
Anarmyt all, as tho it was the gyss,
And thus the King he salust one this wiss.

"Shir King, oneto yow am Y sende
Frome the worthiest that in world is kend
That levyth now of his tyme and age,
Of manhed, wisdome, and of hie curag,
Galiot, sone of the fare Gyande.
And thus, at short, he bidis yow your londe
Ye yald hyme ovr, without impedyment
Or of hyme holde, and if tribut and rent.
This is my charge at short, whilk if youe lest
For to fulfill, of al he haith conquest
He sais that he most tendir shal youe hald."
By short avys the King his ansuer yald:
"Schir knycht, your lorde wondir hie pretendis
When he to me sic salutatioune sendis;
For I as yit, in tymys that ar gone,
Held never lond excep of God alone
Nore never thinkith til erthly lord to yef
Trybut nor rent, als long as I may lef."
"Well," quod the knycht, "ful sor repentith me;
Non may recist the thing the wich mone bee.
To yow, sir King, than frome my lord am I
With diffyans sent, and be this resone why:
His purpos is, or this day moneth day,
With all his ost, planly to assay
Your lond with mony manly man of were
And helmyt knychtis, boith with sheld and spere

And never thinkith to retwrn home whill
That he this lond haith conquest at his will
And ek Uanour the Quen, of whome that hee
Herith report of al this world that shee
In fairhed and in vertew doith excede,
He bad me say he thinkis to possede."
"Schir," quod the King, "your mesag me behufis
Of resone and of curtasy excuss;
But tueching to your lord and to his ost,
His powar, his mesag and his bost,
That pretendith my lond for to distroy,
Tharof as yit tak I non anoye;
And say your lord one my behalf, when hee
Haith tone my lond, that al the world shal see
That it shal be magré myne entent."
With that the knycht, withouten leif, is went,
And richt as he was pasing to the dure
He saith, "A Gode! What wykyt adventure
Apperith!" With that his hors he nome--
Two knichtis kepit, waiting his outcome.
The knicht is gon; the King he gan inquere
At Gawan and at other knychtis sere
If that thei knew or ever hard recorde
Of Galiot, and wharof he wes lorde.
And ther was non among his knychtis all
Which ansuerd o word into the hall.
Than Galygantynis of Walys rase,
That travelit in diverss londis has,
In mony knychtly aventur haith ben.
And to the King he saith, "Sir, I have sen
Galiot, which is the farest knycht
And hiest be half a fut one hycht
That ever I saw, and ek his men accordith;

Hym lakid nocht that to a lord recordith.
For uisare of his ag is non than hee
And ful of larges and humylytee.
An hart he haith of pasing hie curag
And is not twenty-four yer of age.
And of his tyme mekil haith conquerit:
Ten kingis at his command ar sterit.
He uith his men so lovit is, Y gess,
That hyme to pless is al ther besynes.
Not say I this, sir, into the entent
That he, nor none wnder the firmament,
Shal pouere have ayane your majestee;
And or thei shuld, this Y sey for mee--
Rather I shall knychtly into feild
Resave my deith anarmyt wnder sheld.
This spek Y lest."The King, ayan the morn,
Haith uarnit huntaris baith with hund and horne
And arly gan oneto the forest ryd
With mony manly knyghtis by his sid
Hyme for to sport and comfort with the dere
Set contrare was the sesone of the yere
His most huntyng was atte wyld bore.
God wot a lustye cuntree was it thoore
In the ilk tyme.Weil long this noble King
Into this lond haith maid his sujornyng.
Frome the Lady was send o mesinger
Of Melyhalt, wich saith one this maner,
As that the story shewith by recorde:

"To yow, sir King, as to hir soveran lorde,
My lady hath me chargit for to say
How that your lond stondith in affray
For Galiot, sone of the fare Gyande,

Enterit is by armys in your land;
And so the lond and cuntré he anoyth
That quhar he goith planly he distroyth
And makith al obeisand to his honde
That nocht is left wnconquest in that lond,
Excep two castellis longing to hir cwre,
Wich to defend she may nocht long endure.
Wharfor, sir, in wordis plan and short,
Ye mon dispone your folk for to support."
"Wel," quod the King, "oneto thi lady say
The neid is myne; I sall it not delay.
But what folk ar thei nemmyt for to bee
That in my lond is cumyne in sich degree?"
"An hundreth thousand boith uith sheld and spere
On hors ar armyt, al redy for the were."
"Wel," quod the King, "and but delay this nycht,
Or than tomorn as that the day is lycht
I shal remuf; ther shal nothing me mak
Impedyment my jorney for to tak."
Than seith his knychtis al with one assent,
"Shir, that is al contrare our entent;
For to your folk this mater is wnwist
And ye ar here ovr few for to recist
Yone power and youre cuntré to defende.
Tharfor abid and for your folk ye send,
That lyk a king and lyk a weriour
Ye may susten in armys your honoure."
"Now," quod the King, "no langer that I yeme
My crowne, my septure, nor my dyademe
Frome that I here ore frome I wnderstand
That ther by fors be entrit in my land
Men of armys, by strenth of vyolens,
If that I mak abid or resydens

Into o place langar than o nycht
For to defend my cuntré and my rycht."
The King that day his mesage haith furth sent
Throuch al his realme and syne to rest is went.
Up goith the morow; wp goith the brycht day;
Wp goith the sone into his fresh aray.
Richt as he spred his bemys frome northest,
The King wprass withouten more arest
And by his awn conseil and entent
His jornaye tuk at short avysment.
And but dulay he goith frome place to place
Whill that he cam nere whare the lady was
And in one plane apone o rever syde
He lichtit doune, and ther he can abide.
And yit with hyme to batell fore to go
Seven thousand fechteris war thei and no mo.

This was the lady, of qwhome befor I tolde
That Lancilot haith into hir kepinge holde,
But for to tell his pasing hevynesse,
His peyne, his sorow, and his gret distresse
Of presone and of loves gret suppris,
It war to long to me for to devys.
When he remembrith one his hevy charge
Of love, wharof he can hyme not discharge,
He wepith and he sorowith in his chere;
And every nyght semyth hyme o yere.
Gret peité was the sorow that he maad,
And to hymeself apone this wiss he saade:

"Qwhat have Y gilt, allace, or qwhat deservit
That thus myne hart shal uondit ben and carvit
One by the suord of double peine and wo?

My comfort and my plesans is ago;
To me is nat that shuld me glaid reservit.

"I curss the tyme of myne nativitee,
Whar in the heven it ordinyd was for me
In all my lyve never til have eess
But for to be example of disess;
And that apperith that every uicht may see.

"Sen thelke tyme that I had sufficians
Of age and chargit thoghtis sufferans,
Nor never I continewite haith o day
Without the payne of thoghtis hard assay;
Thus goith my youth in tempest and penans.

"And now my body is in presone broght,
But of my wo, that in regard is noght,
The wich myne hart felith evermore.
O deth, allace! Whi hath yow me forbore
That of remed haith the so long besoght?"

Thus nevermore he sesith to compleine,
This woful knyght that felith not bot peine
So prekith hyme the smert of loves sore
And every day encressith more and more.
And with this lady takine is also
And kepit whar he may nowhare go
To haunt knychthed, the wich he most desirit.
And thus his hart with dowbil wo yfirite
We lat hyme duel here with the lady still
Whar he haith laisere for to compleine his fyll.

And Galiot in this meynetyme he laie

By strong myght o castell to assay
With many engyne and diverss wais sere
For of fute folk he had a gret powere
That bowis bur and uther instrumentis,
And with them lede ther palyonis and ther tentis,
With mony o strong chariot and cher
With yrne qwhelis and barris long and sqwar,
Well stuffit with al maner apparell
That longith to o sege or to batell,
Wharwith his ost was closit al about
That of no strenth nedith hyme to dout.
And when he hard the cumyne of the King
And of his ost and of his gaderyng,
The wich he reput but of febil myght
Ayanis hyme for to susten the ficht,
His consell holl assemblit he, but were,
Ten kingis with other lordis sere,
And told theme of the cuming of the King
And askit them there consell of that thing.
Hyme thoght that it his worship wold degrade
If he hymeself in propir persone raide
Enarmyt ayane so few menyé
As it was told Arthur fore to bee.
And thane the Kyng An Hundereth Knychtis cold
(And so he hot, for nevermore he wolde
Ryd of his lond but in his cumpany
O hundyre knyghtis ful of chivellry),
He saith, "Shir, ande I one hond tak,
If it you pless, this jorney shal I mak."
Quod Galiot, "I grant it yow, but ye
Shal first go ryd, yone knychtis ost and see."
Withouten more he ridith ovr the plan
And saw the ost and is returnyd ayann

And callit them mo than he hade sen, forwhy
He dred the reprefe of his cumpany.
And to his lord apone this wys saith hee:
"Shir, ten thousand Y ges them for to bee."
And Galiot haith chargit hyme to tak
Als fell folk and for the feld hyme mak.
And so he doith and haith them wel arayt;
Apone the morne his banaris war displayt.

Up goth the trumpetis with the clariouns;
Ayaine the feld blawen furth ther sownis,
Furth goth this king with al his ost anon.
Be this the word wes to King Arthur gone,
That knew nothing, nor wist of ther entent;
But sone his folk ar oneto armys went.
But Arthur by report hard saye
How Galiot non armys bur that day;
Wharfor he thoght of armys nor of sheld
None wald he tak, nor mak hyme for the feld.
But Gawane haith he clepit, was hyme by,
In qwhome rignith the flour of chevelry,
And told one what maner and one what wyss
He shuld his batelles ordand and devys,
Beseching hyme wisly to forsee
Againe thei folk, wich was far mo than hee.
He knew the charg and passith one his way
Furth to his horss and makith no dulay.
The clariounis blew and furth goth al ononn
And ovr the watter and the furd ar gonne.
Within o playne upone that other syd,
Ther Gawan gon his batellis to devide,
As he wel couth, and set them in aray,
Syne with o manly contynans can say,

"Ye falowis wich of the Round Table benn,
Through al this erth whois fam is hard and sen,
Remembrith now it stondith one the poynt,
Forwhy it lyith one your speris poynt,
The wellfare of the King and of our londe;
And sen the sucour lyith in your honde
And hardement is thing shall most availl
Frome deth ther men of armys in bataill,
Lat now your manhed and your hie curage
The pryd of al thir multitude assuage;
Deth or defence, non other thing we wot."
This fresch king, that Maleginis was hot,
With al his ost he cummyne ovr the plann;
And Gawan send o batell hyme agann
In myde the berde, and festinit in the stell
The sperithis poynt, that bitith scharp and well;
Bot al to few thei war and mycht nocht lest
This gret rout that cummyth one so fast.
Than haith Sir Gawan send, them to support,
One othir batell with one knychtly sorte,
And syne the thrid, and syne the ferde also;
And syne hymeself oneto the feld can go
When that he sauch thar latter batell steir,
And the ten thousand cummyne, al thei ueir.
Qwhar that of armes previt he so well,
His ennemys gane his mortall strokis fell.
He goith ymong them in his hie curage
As he that had of knyghthed the wsage
And couth hyme weill conten into o shour;
Againe his strok resistit non armour.
And mony knycht that worth ware and bolde
War thore with hyme of Arthuris houshold
And knyghtly gan oneto the feld them bere,

And mekil wroght of armys into were.
Sir Gawan than upone such wyss hyme bure,
This othere goith al to discumfitoure.
Sevyne thousand fled and of the feld thei go,
Wharof this king into his hart was wo,
For of hymeself he was of hie curage.
To Galiot than send he in mesag
That he shuld help his folk for to defende
And he to hyme hath thirté thousand sende,
Wharof this king gladith in his hart
And thinkith to reveng all the smart
That he tofor haith suffirit and the payne.
And al his folk returnyt is ayayne
Atour the feld and cummyne thilk as haill.
The swyft horss goith first to the assall.
This noble knyght that seith the grete forss
Of armyt men that cummyne upone horss
Togiddir semblit al his falowschip
And thoght them at the sharp poynt to kep
So that thar harmm shal be ful deir yboght.
This uthere folk with straucht courss hath socht
Out of aray atour the larg felld.
Thar was the strokis festnit in the shelde
Thei war resavit at the speris end.
So Arthuris folk can manfully defend;
The formest can thar lyves end conclude.
Whar sone assemblit al the multitude,
Thar was defens, ther was gret assaill;
Richt wonderfull and strong was the bataill
Whar Arthuris folk sustenit mekil payn
And knychtly them defendit haith againe.
Bot endur thei mycht apone no wyss
The multitude and ek the gret suppriss.

But Gawan, wich that setith al his payn
Upone knyghthed, defendid so againe
That only in the manhede of this knyght
His folk rejosit them of his gret myght,
And ek abasit hath his ennemys;
For throw the feld he goith in such wyss
And in the press so manfully them servith
His suerd atwo the helmys al tokervith,
The hedis of he be the shouderis smat;
The horss goith, of the maister desolat.
But what avaleth al his besynes,
So strong and so insufferable uas the press?
His folk are passit atour the furdis ilkon,
Towart ther bretis and to ther luges gon,
Whar he and many worthy knyght also
Of Arthuris houss endurit mekill wo
That never men mar into armys uroght
Of manhed; yit was it al for noght.
Thar was the strenth, ther was the pasing myght
Of Gawan, wich that whill the dirk nyght
Befor the luges faucht al hyme alonn,
When that his falowis entrit ware ilkonn,
On Arthuris half war mony tan and slan.
And Galotis folk is hame returnyd againe,
For it was lait. Away the ostis ridith,
And Gawan yit apone his horss abidith
With suerd in hond when thei away uar gon;
And so forwrocht hys lymmys uer ilkon
And wondit ek his body up and doune,
Upone his horss right thore he fel in swoune.
And thei hyme tuk and to his lugyne bare.
Boith King and Qwen of hyme uare in dispare;
For thei supposit, throw marvellis that he uroght,

He had hymeself to his confusioune broght.

This was nereby of Melyhalt, the hyll
Whar Lanscelot yit was with the lady still.
The knychtis of the court pasing homme;
This ladiis knychtis to hir palice com
And told to hir how that the feld was uent
And of Gawan and of his hardyment
That mervell was his manhed to behold.
And sone thir tithingis to the knycht uas told
That was with wo and hevyness opprest,
So noyith hyme his sujorne and his rest.
And but dulay one for o knycht he send
That was most speciall with the lady kend.
He comyne and the knycht unto hyme said,
"Displess you not, sir, be yhe not ill paid,
So homly thus I yow exort to go
To gare my lady spek o word or two
With me that am a carful presonere."
"Sir, your commande Y shall, withouten were,
Fulfill."And to his lady passit hee,
In lawly wyss besiching hir that she
Wald grant hyme to pas at his request
Unto hir knycht stood wnder hir arest.
And she, that knew al gentilless aright,
Furth to his chamber passit wight the licht.

And he aross and salust curtasly
The lady and said, "Madem, her I,
Your presoner, besekith yow that yhe
Wold mersy and compassione have of me
And mak the ransone wich that I may yeif.
I waist my tyme in presone thus to leife

Forwhy I her on be report be-told
That Arthur, with the flour of his housholde,
Is cummyne here and in this cuntré lyis
And stant in danger of his ennemyis
And haith assemblit; and eft this shalt bee
Within short tyme one new assemblee.
Tharfor, my lady, Y youe grace besech
That I mycht pas, my ranson for to fech,
Fore I presume thar longith to that sort
That lovid me and shal my nede support."

"Shire knycht, it stant nocht in sich dugree;
It is no ransone wich that causith
To holden yow or don yow sich offens.
It is your gilt, it is your violens
Wharof that I desir nothing but law,
Without report, your awnn trespas to knaw."
"Madem, your plesance may ye wel fulfill
Of me that am in presone at your will.
Bot of that gilt I was for til excuss
For that I did of verrey nede behwss--
It tuechit to my honore and my fame;
I mycht nocht lefe it but hurting of my nam,
And ek the knycht was mor to blam than I.
But ye, my lady, of your curtessy,
Wold ye deden my ransone to resave
Of presone so I my libertee myght have,
Y ware yolde evermore your knyght
Whill that I leif with al my holl myght.
And if so be ye lykith not to ma
My ransone, if me leif to ga
To the assemblé, wich sal be of new;
And, as that I am feithful knycht and trew,

At nycht to yow I enter shall againe--
But if that deth or other lat certann,
Throw wich I have such impediment
That I be hold, magré myne entent."
"Sir knycht," quod she, "I grant yow leif, withthy
Your name to me that ye wil specify."
"Madem, as yit sutly I ne may
Duclar my name, one be no maner way;
But I promyt, als fast as I have tyme
Convenient or may uithouten cryme,
I shall."And than the lady saith hyme tyll,
"And I, schir knycht, one this condiscione will
Grant yow leve, so that ye oblist bee
For to return as ye have said to me."
Thus thei accord.The lady goith to rest.
The sone discending closit in the uest.
The ferd day was devysit for to bee
Betuex the ostis of the assemblee.

And Galiot richt arly by the day
Ayane the feld he can his folk aray.
And fourty thousand armyt men haith he
That war not at the othir assemblé
Commandit to the batell for to gon.
"And I myself," quod he, "shal me dispone
Onto the feild againe the thrid day,
Wharof this were we shal the end assay."

And Arthuris folk that come one every syd,
He for the feld can them for to provide,
Wich ware to few againe the gret affere
Of Galiot yit to susten the were.
The knychtis al out of the ceté ross

Of Melyholt, and to the semblé gois.
And the lady haith, into sacret wyss,
Gart for hir knycht and presoner dewyss
In red al thing that ganith for the were:
His curseir red, so was boith scheld and spere.
And he to qwham the presone hath ben smart
With glaid desir apone his cursour start.
Towart the feld anon he gan to ryd
And in o plan hovit one rever syde.
This knycht, the wich that long haith ben in cag,
He grew into o fresch and new curage,
Seing the morow blythfull and amen,
The med, the rever and the uodis gren,
The knychtis in armys them arayinge,
The baneris ayaine the feld displayng.
His youth in strenth and in prosperytee
And syne of lust the gret adversytee,
Thus in his thocht remembryng at the last
Efterward one syd he gan his ey to cast
Whar ovr a bertes lying haith he sen
Out to the feld luking was the Qwen.
Sudandly with that his gost astart
Of love anone haith caucht hyme by the hart.
Than saith he, "How long shall it be so,
Love, at yow shall wirk me al this wo,
Apone this wyss to be infortunat,
Hir for to serve the wich thei no thing wate
What sufferance I in hir wo endure
Nor of my wo nor of myne adventure?
And I wnworthy ame for to attane
To hir presens nor dare I noght complane.
Bot, hart, sen at yow knawith she is here
That of thi lyve and of thi deith is stere,

Now is thi tyme, now help thiself at neid
And the devod of every point of dred
That cowardy be none into the senn;
Fore and yow do, yow knowis thi peyne, I weyn.
Yow art wnable ever to attane
To hir mercy or cum be ony mayne.
Tharfor Y red hir thonk at yow disserve
Or in hir presens lyk o knycht to sterf."
With that confusit with an hevy thocht
Which ner his deith ful oft tyme haith hyme socht,
Devoydit was his spritis and his gost,
He wist not of hymeself nor of his ost
Bot one his horss, als still as ony ston.
When that the knychtis armyt war ilkon,
To warnnyng them up goith the bludy sown
And every knyght upone his horss is bown,
Twenty thousand armyt men of were.
The King that day he wold non armys bere;
His batellis ware devysit everilkon
And them forbad out ovr the furdis to gon.
Bot frome that thei ther ennemys haith sen,
Into such wys thei couth them noght sustenn.
Bot ovr thei went uithouten more delay
And can them one that other sid assay.
The Red Knycht still into his hevy thoght
Was hufying yit apone the furd and noght
Wist of himeself; with that a harrold com
And sone the knycht he be the brydill nom
Saying, "Awalk! It is no tyme to slep.
Your worschip more expedient uare to kep."
No word he spak, so prikith hyme the smart
Of hevynes that stood unto his hart.
Two screwis cam with that, of quhich onn

The knychtis sheld rycht frome his hals haith tonn;
That uthir watter takith atte last
And in the knychtis ventail haith it cast.
When that he felt the uatter that uas cold,
He wonk and gan about hyme to behold
And thinkith how he sumquhat haith mysgonn.
With that his spere into his hand haith ton,
Goith to the feild withouten uordis more.
So was he uare whare that there cam before,
O manly man he was into al thing
And clepit was the Ferst-Conquest King.
The Red Knycht with spuris smat the sted;
The tother cam that of hyme hath no drede.
With ferss curag ben the knychtis met.
The king his spere apone the knycht hath set
That al in peciss flaw into the felde.
His hawbrek helpit, suppos he had no scheld.
And he the king into the scheld haith ton
That horss and man boith to the erd ar gon.
Than to the knycht he cummyth, that haith tan
His sheld, to hyme deliverith it ayane,
Besiching hyme that of his ignorance,
That knew hyme nat, as takith no grevance.
The knycht his scheld but mor delay haith tak
And let hyme go and nothing to hyme spak.
Than thei the wich that so at erth haith sen
Ther lord, the Ferst-Conquest King, Y menn,
In haist thei cam, as that thei uar agrevit;
And manfully thei haith ther King relevit.

And Arthuris folk, that lykith not to byde,
In goith the spuris in the stedis syde.
Togiddir thar assemblit al the ost,

At whois meting many o knycht was lost.

The batell was richt crewell to behold,

Of knychtis wich that haith there lyvis yolde.

Oneto the hart the spere goith throw the scheld;

The knychtis gaping lyith in the feld.

The Red Knycht, byrnyng in loves fyre,

Goith to o knycht als swift as ony vyre,

The wich he persit throuch and throuch the hart.

The spere is went; with that anon he start

And out o suerd into his hond he tais.

Lyk to o lyone into the feld he gais,

Into his rag smyting to and fro:

Fro sum the arm, fro sum the nek in two;

Sum in the feild lying is in swoun,

And sum his suerd goith to the belt al dounne.

For qwhen that he beholdith to the Qwen,

Who had ben thore his manhed to have sen,

His doing into armys and his myght,

Shwld say in world war not such o wight.

His falouschip siche comfort of his dede

Haith ton that thei ther ennemys ne dreid

But can themself ay manfoly conten

Into the stour that hard was to susten.

For Galyot was o pasing multitude

Of previt men in armys that war gude,

The wich can with o fresch curag assaill

Ther ennemys that day into batell,

That ne ware not the uorschip and manhede

Of the Red Knycht, in perell and in dreid

Arthuris folk had ben, uithouten uere.

Set thei uar good, thei uar of smal powere.

And Gawan, wich gart bryng hymeself befor

To the bertes, set he was uondit sore,

Whar the Qwen uas and whar that he mycht see
The manere of the ost and assemblé.
And when that he the gret manhed haith sen
Of the Red Knycht, he saith oneto the Qwen,
"Madem, yone knycht into the armys rede,
Nor never I hard nore saw into no sted
O knycht, the wich that into schortar space
In armys haith mor forton nore mor grace,
Nore bettir doith boith with sper and scheild;
He is the hed and comfort of our feild."
"Now, sir, I traist that never more uas sen
No man in feild more knyghtly hyme conten.
I pray to Hyme that everything hath cure,
Saif hyme fro deth or wykit adventure."
The feild it was rycht perellus and strong
On boith the sydis and continewit long,
Ay from the sone the uarldis face gan licht
Whill he was gone and cumyne uas the nycht.
And than o forss thei mycht it not asstart:
On every syd behovit them depart.
The feild is don and ham goith every knycht;
And prevaly, unwist of any wicht,
The way the Red Knycht to the ceté taiis,
As he had hecht, and in his chambre gais.
When Arthure hard how the knycht is gon,
He blamyt sore his lordis everilkone;
And oft he haith remembrit in his thoght
What multitud that Galiot had broght.
Seing his folk that ware so evil arayt,
Into his mynd he stondith al affrayt
And saith, "I traist ful suth it sal be founde,
My drem richt as the clerkis gan expounde;
Forwhy my men failyeis now at neid

Myself, my londe, in perell and in dreide."

And Galiot upone hie worschip set,
And his consell anon he gart be fet.
To them he saith, "With Arthur weil ye see
How that it stant and to qwhat degré,
Aganis ws that he is no poware.
Wharfor, me think, no worschip to ws ware
In conqueryng of hyme nor of his londe;
He haith no strenth, he may ws not uithstonde.
Wharfor, me think it best is to delay
And resput hyme for a tuelmonneth day
Whill that he may assemble al his myght;
Than is mor worschip aganis hyme to ficht."
And thus concludit, thoght hyme for the best.
The uery knychtis passing to there rest;
Of Melyholt the ladeis knychtis ilkone
Went home and to hir presens ar thei gon,
At qwhome ful sone than gan scho to inquere
And al the maner of the ostis till spere:
How that it went and in what maner wyss,
Who haith most worschip and who is most to pryss.
"Madem," quod thei, "o knycht was in the
Of red was al his armour and his shield--
Whois manhed can al otheris exced; feild
May nan report in armys half his deid;
Ne wor his worschip, shortly to conclud,
Our folk of help had ben al destitud.
He haith the thonk, the uorschip in hyme lyis
That we the feld defendit in sich wyss."
The lady thane oneto hirself haith thocht,
"Whether is yone my presonar ore noght,
The suthfastness that shal Y wit onon."

When every wight unto ther rest war gon
She clepith one hir cwsynes ful nere,
Wich was to hir most speciall and dere,
And saith to hir, "Qwhethar if yone bee
Our presoner, my consell is we see."
With that the maden in hir hand hath ton
O torche and to the stabille ar thei gon
And fond his sted lying at the ground,
Wich wery was, ywet with mony wounde.
The maden saith, "Upone this horss is sen
He in the place quhar strokis was hath benn;
And yhit the horss, it is nocht wich that hee
Furth with hyme hade," the lady said; "per Dee,
He usyt haith mo horss than one or two.
I red oneto his armys at we go."
Tharwith oneto his armys ar thei went.
Thei fond his helm, thei fond his hawbrek rent;
Thei fond his scheld was fruschit al to nocht.
At schort, his armour in sich wyss uas urocht
In every place that no thing was left haill
Nore never eft accordith to bataill.
Than saith the lady to hir cusyness,
"What sal we say, what of this mater gess?"
"Madem, I say thei have nocht ben abwsyt;
He that them bur, schortly he has them usyt."
"That may ye say, suppos the best that levis
Or most of worschip intil armys previs
Or yhit haith ben in ony tyme befornn,
Had them in feld, in his mast curag, bornn."
"Now," quod the lady, "will we pass and see
The knycht hymeself and ther the suth may we
Knaw of this thing."Incontynent them boith
Thir ladeis unto his chambre goith.

The knycht al wery fallyng was on slep;
This maden passith in and takith kep.
Sche sauch his brest with al his schowderis bare
That bludy war and woundit her and thare.
His face was al tohurt and al toschent;
His nevis swellyng war and al torent.
Sche smylyt a lyt and to hir lady said,
"It semyth weill this knycht hath ben assaid."
The lady sauch and rewit in hir thoght
The knychtis worschip wich that he haith uroght.
In hire remembrance Loves fyré dart
With hot desyre hir smat oneto the hart.
And than a quhill, withouten wordis mo,
Into hir mynd thinking to and fro,
She studeit so and at the last abraid
Out of hir thocht and sudandly thus said.
"Withdraw," quod she, "one syd a lyt the lyght
Or that I pass that I may kyss the knyght."
"Madem," quod sche, "what is it at ye menn?
Of hie worschip ovr mekill have ye senn
So sone to be supprisit with o thoght.
What is it at yhe think?Preswm ye noght
That if yon knycht wil walkin and persaif
He shal tharof nothing bot evill consaif,
In his entent ruput yow therby
The ablare to al lychtness and foly?
And blam the more al utheris in his mynd
If your gret wit in sich desire he fynde?"
"Nay," quod the lady, "nothing may I do,
For sich o knycht may be defam me to."
"Madem, I wot that for to love yone knycht--
Considir his fame, his worschip and his mycht--
And to begyne as worschip wil devyss,

Syne he ayaine mycht love yow one such wyss
And hold yow for his lady and his love,
It war to yow no maner of reprwe.
But quhat if he appelit be and thret
His hart to love and elliswhar yset?
And wel Y wot, madem, if it be so,
His hart hyme sal not suffir to love two,
For noble hart wil have no dowbilness.
If it be so, yhe tyne yowr lov, I gess.
Than is yourself, than is your love refusit,
Your fam is hurt, your gladness is conclusit.
My consell is therfore you to absten
Whill that to yow the verray rycht be senn
Of his entent, the wich ful son yhe may
Have knawlag if yow lykith to assay."
So mokil to hir lady haith she uroght
That at that tyme she haith returnyt hir thocht
And to hir chambre went, withouten more,
Whar love of new assaith hir ful sore.
So well long thei speking of the knycht,
Hir cusynace hath don al at she mycht
For to expel that thing out of hir thocht.
It wil not be.Hir labour is for nocht.
Now leif we hir into hir newest pan,
And to Arthur we wil retwrn agann.

BOOK 2

The clowdy nyght, wndir whois obscure
The rest and quiet of every criatur
Lyith sauf, quhare the gost with besyness
Is occupiit with thoghtfull hevynes.
And, for that thocht furth schewing uil his mycht,
Go farewel rest and quiet of the nycht.
Artur, I meyne, to whome that rest is nocht,
But al the nycht supprisit is with thocht.
Into his bed he turnyth to and fro,
Remembryng the apperans of his wo,
That is to say, his deith, his confusioune,
And of his realme the opin distruccioune,
That in his wit he can nothing provide
Bot tak his forton thar for to abyd.
Up goith the son, up goith the hot morow.
The thoghtful King, al the nycht to sorow,
That sauch the day, upone his feit he start,
And furth he goith, distrublit in his hart.
A quhill he walkith in his pensyf gost,
So was he ware thar cummyne to the ost

O clerk, with whome he was aqwynt befor--
Into his tyme non better was ybore--
Of qwhois com he gretly uas rejosit,
For into hyme sum comfort he supposit.
Betuex them was one hartly affeccioune.
Non orderis had he of relegioune;
Famus he was and of gret excellence
And rycht expert in al the seven science,
Contemplatif and chast in governance,
And clepit was the Maister Amytans.
The King befor his palyoune one the gren,
That knew hyme well and haith his cummyn senn
Uelcummyt hyme and maid hyme rycht gud chere.
And he agan, agrevit as he were,
Saith, "Nothir of thi salosing nor the
Ne rak I nocht, ne charg I nocht," quod hee.
Than quod the King, "Maister, and for what why
Are ye agrevit or quhat tresspas have I
Commytit so that I shal yow disples?"
Quod he, "Nothing it is ayane myn ess
But only contrare of thiself alway,
So fare the courss yow passith of the way.
Thi schip that goth apone the stormy uall,
Ney of thi careldis, in the swelf it fall
Whar she almost is in the perell drent;
That is to say, yow art so far myswent
Of wykitness upone the urechit dans
That yow art fallyng in the storng vengans
Of Goddis wreth that shal the son devour.
For of His strok approchit now the hour
That boith thi ringe, thi ceptre and thi crounn
From hie estat He smyting shal adoune.
And that accordith well, for in thi thocht

Yow knawith not Hyme, the wich that haith the
    wrocht
And set the up into this hie estat
From povert. For, as theselvyne wat,
It cummyth al bot only of His myght
And not of the nor of thi elderis richt
To the discending as in heritage,
For yow was not byget onto spousag.
Wharfor yow aucht His biding to obserf,
And at thy mycht yow shuld Hyme pless and serf.
That dois yow nat, for yow art so confussit
With this fals warld that thow haith Hyme refusit
And brokine haith His reul and ordynans,
The wich to the He gave in governans.
He maid the King, He maid the governour,
He maid the so and set in hie honour
Of realmys and of peplis sere;
Efter His love thow shuld them reul and stere
And wnoppressit kep into justice
The wykit men and pwnyce for ther vice.
Yow dois nothing bot al in the contrare
And suffrith al thi puple to forfare.
Yow haith non ey bot one thyne awn delyt
Or quhat that plesing shall thyne appetyt.
In the defalt of law and of justice,
Wndir thi hond is sufferyt gret suppriss
Of fadirless and modirless also,
And wedwis ek sustenit mekill wo.
With gret myschef oppressit ar the pure;
And thow art causs of al this hol injure,
Wharof that God a raknyng sal craf
At the, and a sore raknyng sal hafe.
For thyne estat is gevyne to redress

Thar ned and kep them to rychtwysness.
And thar is non that ther complantis heris;
The mychty folk and ek the flattereris
Ar cheif with the and doith this oppressioun.
If thai complen, it is ther confussioune.
And Daniell saith that who doith to the pure
Or faderless or modirless, enjure
Or to the puple that ilke to God doth hee;
And al this harme sustenit is throw the.
Yow sufferith them, oppressith and anoyith.
So yow art causs; throw the thei ar distroyth.
Than, at thi mycht, God so distroys yow.
What shal He do agane? Quhat shal yow
When he distroys by vengance of his suerd
The synaris fra the vysagis of the erde?
Than utraly yow shall distroyt bee;
And that richt weill apperis now of thee,
For yow allon byleft art solitere.
And the wyss Salamon can duclar,
'Wo be to hyme that is byleft alone;
He haith no help.' So is thi forton gonne.
For he is callit, with quhom that God is nocht,
Allone. And so thi wykitness haith wrocht
That God Hymeself, He is bycummyn thi fo.
Thi pupleis hartis haith thow tynt also.
Thi wykitness thus haith the maid alon
That of this erth thi fortone is ygonn.
Yow mone thi lyf yow mone thi uorschip tyne
And eft to deth that never shal haf fyne."

"Maister," quod he, "of yowre benevolens
Y yow besech that tueching myn offens
Yhe wald vichsaif your consell to me if

How I sal mend and ek hereftir leif."
"Now, quod the Maister, "and I have mervell qwhy
Yow askith consail and wil in non affy
Nor wyrk tharby; and yhit yow may in tym,
If yow lykith to, amend the cryme."
"Yhis," saith the King, "and suthfastly I will
Your ordynans in everything fulfyll."
"And if the list at consail to abide,
The remed of thi harme to provyde,
First, the begyning is of sapiens
To dreid the Lord and His magnificens.
And what thow haith in contrar Hyme ofendit,
Whill yow haith mycht, of fre desir amendit.
Repent thi gilt, repent thi gret trespass;
And remembir one Goddis richwysness,
How for to Hyme that wykitness anoyt
And how the way of synaris He distroit.
And if ye lyk to ryng wnder his pess
The vengans of His mychty hond yow sess,
This schalt yow do, if yow wil be perfit.
First mone yow be penitent and contrit
Of everything that tuechith thi consiens,
Done of fre will or yhit of neglygens.
Thi neid requirith ful contretioune,
Princepaly, without conclusioune.
With humble hart and gostly bysyness,
Syne shalt yow go devotly the confess
Therof unto sum haly conffessour
That the wil consail tueching thin arour,
And to fulfill his will and ordynans
In satisfaccione and doing of pennans,
And to amend al wrang and al injure
By the ydone til every creature,

If yow can into thi hart fynde
Contretioune, well degest into thi mynd.
Now go thi weie, for if it leful were
Confessioune to me, I shuld it here."

Than Arthur, richt obedient and mek,
Into his wit memoratyve can seik
Of every gilt wich that he can pens
Done frome he passith the yeris of innocens;
And as his Maister hyme commandit hade,
He goith and his confessione haith he maad
Richt devotly with lementable chere.
The maner wich quho lykith for to here
He may it fynd into the holl romans.
Off confessione o pasing cercumstans
I can it not; I am no confessour.
My wyt haith evil consat of that labour,
Quharof I wot I aucht repent me sore.
The King wich was confessit, what is more,
Goith and til his Maister tellith hee
How every syne into his awn degree
He shew that mycht occuryng to his mynde.
"Now," quod the Maistere, "left thow aght behynde
Of Albenak the uorschipful King Ban,
The wich that uas into thy service slan,
And of his wif disherist eft also?
Bot of ther sone, the wich was them fro,
Ne spek Y not." The King in his entent
Abasyt was and furthwith is he went
Agane and to his confessour declarith.
Syne to his Maister he ayane reparith,
To quhome he saith, "I aftir my cunyng
Your ordinans fulfillit in al thing.

And now right hartly Y beseich and prey
Yhe wald vithschaif sumthing to me say
That may me comfort in my gret dreid
And how my men ar falyet in my neid
And of my dreme, the wich that is so dirk."
This Maister saith, "And thow art bound to uirk

At my consail, and if yow has maad
Thi confessione, as yow before hath said,
And in thi conciens thinkith persevere,
As I presume that thow onon shalt here
That God Hymeself shal so for the provide,
Thow shal remayne and in thi ring abyd.
And why thi men ar falyet at this nede,
At short this is the causs, shalt yow nocht dred,
Fore yow to Gode was frawart and perwert.
Thi ryngne and the He thocht for to subvart.
And yow sal knaw na power may recist
In contrar quhat God lykith to assist.
The vertw nore the strenth of victory,
It cummyth not of man, bot anerly
Of Hyme, the wich haith every strinth; and than
If that the waiis plessit Hyme of man,
He shal have forss againe his ennemys.
Aryght agan apone the samyne uyss,
If he displess unto the Lord, he shall
Be to his fais a subjet or a thrall,
As that we may into the Bible red
Tueching the folk He tuk Hymeself to led
Into the lond, the wich He them byhicht.
Ay when thei yhed into His ways richt,
Ther fois gon befor there suerd to nocht;
And when that thei ayanis Hyme hath urocht,

Thei war so full of radur and disspare
That of o leif fleing in the air,
The sound of it haith gart o thousand tak
At onys apone themself the bak
And al ther manhed uterly foryhet,
Sich dreid the Lord apone ther hartis set.
So shalt yow know no powar may withstond
Ther God Hymeself hath ton the causs on hond.
And the quhy stant in thyne awn offens
That al thi puple falyhet off defens.
And sum are falyeing magré ther entent;
Thei ar to quhom yow yevyne hath thi rent,
Thi gret reuard, thi richess and thi gold
And cherissith and held in thi houshold.
Bot the most part ar falyheit the at wyll,
To quhome yow haith wnkyndness schawin till,
Wrong and injure and ek defalt of law
And pwnysing of qwhich that thei stand aw,
And makith service but reward or fee,
Syne haith no thonk bot fremmytness of the.
Such folk to the cummyth bot for dred,
Not of fre hart the for to help at nede.
And what avalith owthir sheld or sper
Or horss or armoure according for the were
Uithouten man them for to stere and led?
And man, yow wot, that uantith hart is ded
That into armys servith he of noght.
A coward oft ful mekil harm haith uroght.
In multitude nore yhit in confluens
Of sich is nowther manhed nore defens.
And so thow hath the rewlyt that almost
Of al thi puple the hartis ben ylost
And tynt richt throw thyne awn mysgovernans

Of averice and of thyne errogans.
What is o prince, quhat is o governoure
Withouten fame of worschip and honour?
What is his mycht, suppos he be a lorde,
If that his folk sal nocht to hyme accorde?
May he his rigne, may he his holl empire
Susten al only of his owne desyre
In servyng of his wrechit appetit
Of averice and of his awn delyt
And hald his men wncherist in thraldome?
Nay! that shal sone his hie estat consome,
For many o knycht therby is broght ydoune
All uteraly to ther confusioune.
For oft it makith uther kingis by
To wer on them in trast of victory.
And oft als throw his peple is distroyth
That fyndith them agrevit or anoyth.
And God also oft with His awn swerd
Punysith ther vysis one this erd.
Thus falith not: o king but governans,
Boith realme and he goith oneto myschans."

As thai war thus speking of this thinge,
Frome Galiot cam two knychtis to the King.
That one the King of Hundereth Knychtis was;
That other to nome "The Fyrst-Conquest King"
    he has
As first that Galyot conquerit of one.
The nerest way oneto the King thei gon,
And up he ross as he that wel couth do
Honor to qwhome that it afferith to.
And yhit he wist not at thei kingis were;
So them thei boith and uyth rycht knyghtly cher

Reverendly thei salust hyme and thane
The King of Hunder Knyghtis he began
And said hyme, "Sir, to yow my lord ws sende,
Galiot, whilk bad ws say he wende
That of this world the uorthiest king wor yhe,
Gretest of men and of awtoritee.
Wharof he has gret wonder that yhe ar
So feblé cummyne into his contrare
For to defend your cuntré and your londe,
And knowith well yhe may hyme nocht withstonde.
Wharfor he thinkith no worschip to conquere
Nore in the weris more to persyvere.
Considdir yowr wakness and yowr indegens,
Aganis hyme as now to mak defens.
Wharfore, my lord haith grantit by us here
Trewis to yhow and resput for o yhere,
If that yhow lykith by the yheris space
For to retwrn ayane into this place,
Her to manteine yhour cuntré and withstand
Hyme with the holl power of yhour lond.
And for the tyme the trewis shal endure,
Yhour cuntré and yhour lond he will assurre;
And wit yhe yhit his powar is nocht here.
And als he bad ws say yhow by the yhere
The gud knycht wich that the red armys bure
And in the feild maid the discumfiture,
The whilk the flour of knychthed may be cold,
He thinkith hyme to have of his houshold."
"Well," quod the King, "I have hard quhat yhe say;
But if God will and ek if that I may,
Into sich wyss I think for to withstond,
Yhour lord shall have no powar of my londe."
Of this mesag the King rejosing hass

And of the trewis wich that grantit was,
Bot anoyt yhit of the knycht was he,
Wich thei avant to have in such dogré.
Ther leif thei tuk, and when at thei war gon,

This Maister saith, "How lykith God dispone
Now may yhow se and suth is my recorde.
For by Hyme now is makith this accord,
And by non uthir worldly providens
Sauf only grant of His bynevolans,
To se if that the lykith to amend
And to provid thi cuntré to defend.
Wharfor yow shalt into thi lond home fair
And governe the as that I shall declaire:
First, thi God with humble hart yow serfe
And his comand at al thi mycht obserf;
And syne, lat pass the ilk blessit wonde
Of lowe with mercy justly throw thi londe.
And Y beseich to qwhome yow sal direke
The rewle upone the wrangis to correk
That yow be nocht in thi electioune blynde;
For writin it is and yow sal trew it fynde
That be thei for to thonk or ellis blame
And towart God thi part shal be the samm;
Of ignorans shalt yow nocht be excusit,
Bot in ther werkis sorly be accusit.
For thow shuld ever chess apone sich wyss
The minsteris that rewll haith of justice:
First, that he be descret til wnderstond
And lowe and ek the mater of the londe,
And be of mycht and ek autoritee--
For puple ay contempnith low degré--
And that of trouth he folow furth the way;

That is als mych as he lovyth trewth alway
And haitith al them the wich sal pas therfro.
Syne, that he God dreid and love also.
Of averice bewar with the desyre,
And of hyme full of hastyness and fyre;
Bewar tharfor of malice and desire
And hyme also that lovith no medyre.
For al this abhominable was hold
When justice was into the tymis olde.
For qwho that is of an of thir byknow,
The lest of them subvertith all the low
And makith it wnjustly to procede.
Eschew tharfor, for this sal be thi meid
Apone the day when al thing goith aright,
Whar none excuss hidyng schal the lyght,
But He the Jug, that no man may susspek,
Everything ful justly sal correk.
Bewar tharwith, as before have I told,
And chess them wysly that thi low shal hold.
And als I will that it well oft be sen,
Richt to thiself how thei thi low conten,
And how the right and how the dom is went
For to inquer that yow be delygent.
And punyss sor, for o thing shal yow know,
The most trespas is to subvert the low,
So that yow be not in thar gilt accusit
And frome the froit of blissit folk refusit.
And pas yow shalt to every chef toune
Throwout the boundis of thi regioune
Whar yow sall be, that justice be elyk
Without divisione baith to pur and ryk.
And that thi puple have awdiens
With thar complantis and also thi presens,

For qwho his eris frome the puple stekith
And not his hond in ther support furth rekith,
His dom sall be ful grevous and ful hard
When he sal cry and he sal nocht be hard.
Wharfor thyne eris ifith to the pwre,
Bot in redress of ned and not of injure.
Thus sall thei don of ressone and knawlag.

"But kingis when thei ben of tender ag,
Y wil not say I trast thei ben excusit,
Bot schortly thei sall be sar accusit
When so thei cum to yheris of resone
If thei tak not full contrisioune
And pwnyss them that hath ther low mysgyit.
That this is trouth it may not be denyit;
For uther ways thei sal them not discharg

. . . .

One estatis of ther realm that shold
Within his youth se that his low be hold.
And thus thow the, with mercy, kep alway
Of justice furth the ilk blessit way.

"And of thi wordis beis trew and stable,
Spek not to mych, nore be not vareable.
O kingis word shuld be o kingis bonde
And said it is, a kingis word shuld stond.
O kingis word, among our faderis old,
Al-out more precious and more sur was hold
Than was the oth or seel of any wight.
O king of trouth suld be the verray lyght,
So treuth and justice to o king accordyth.
And als, as thir clerkis old recordith,
"In tyme is larges and humilitee

Right well according unto hie dugré
And plessith boith to God and man also.
Wharfor I wil incontinent thow go
And of thi lond in every part abide,
Whar yow gar fet and clep one every sid
Out of thi cuntreis and ek out of thi tounis,
Thi dukis, erlis and thi gret baronis,
Thi pur knychtis and thi bachleris,
And them resauf als hartly as afferis
And be themself yow welcum them ilkon.
Syne, them to glaid and cheris, thee dispone
With festing and with humyll contynans.
Be not pensyve, nore proud in arrogans,
Bot with them hold in gladnes cumpany.
Not with the rich nor myghty anerly,
Bot with the pure worthi man also,
With them thow sit, with them yow ryd and go.
I say not to be ovr fameliar,
For, as the most philosephur can duclar,
To mych to oyss familiaritee
Contempnyng bryngith oneto hie dugré;
Bot cherice them with wordis fair depaynt,
So with thi pupelle sal yow the aquaynt.
Than of ilk cuntré wysly yow enquere
An agit knycht to be thi consulere,
That haith ben hold in armys richt famus,
Wyss and discret, and nothing invyus.
For there is non that knowith so wel, iwyss,
O worthy man as he that worthi is.
When well long haith yow swjornyt in a place
And well acqueynt the uith thi puple has,
Than shalt thow ordand and provid the
Of horss and ek of armour gret plenté,

Of gold and silver, tressore and cleithing,
And every riches that longith to o king.
And when the lykith for to tak thi leif,
By largess thus yow thi reward geif,
First to the pure worthy honorable
That is til armys and til manhed able.
Set he be pur, yhit worschip in hyme bidith.
If hyme the horss one wich thiselvyne ridith
And bid hyme that he rid hyme for yhour sak;
Syne til hyme gold and silver yow betak:
The horss to hyme for worschip and prowes,
The tresor for his fredome and larges.
If most of riches and of cherising
Eftir this gud knycht berith uitnesing.
Syne to thi tennandis and to thi vavasouris
If essy haknays, palfrais and cursouris,
And robis sich as plesand ben and fair.
Syne to thi lordis, wich at mychty aire,
As dukis, erlis, princis and ek kingis,
Yow if them strang, yow if them uncouth thingis,
As diverss jowellis and ek preciouss stonis,
Or halkis, hundis, ordinit for the nonis,
Or wantone horss that can nocht stand in stable.
Thar giftis mot be fair and delitable.
Thus first unto the uorthi pur yow if
Giftis that may ther poverté releif,
And to the rich iftis of plesans--
That thei be fair, set nocht of gret substans.
For riches askith nothing bot delyt,
And povert haith ay ane appetyt,
For to support ther ned and indigens.
Thus shall yow if and makith thi dispens.
And ek the Quen, my lady, shalt also

To madenis and to ladeis, quhar yhe go,
If and cheriss one the samyne wyss;
For into largess al thi welfar lyis.
And if thi giftis with sich continans
That thei be sen ay gifyne uith plesans.
The wyss man sais, and suth it is approvit,
Thar is no thonk, thar is no ift alowit,
Bot it be ifyne into sich manere--
That is to say, als glaid into his chere--
As he the wich the ift of hyme resavith;
And do he not, the gifar is dissavith.
For who that iffis as he not if wald,
Mor profit war his ift for to withhald.
His thonk he tynith and his ift also.
Bot that thow ifith, if with boith two,
That is to say, uith hart and hand atonis.
And so the wys man ay the ift disponis.
Beith larg and iffis frely of thi thing,
For largess is the tresour of o king
And not this other jowellis nor this gold
That is into thi tresory withholde.
Who gladly iffith, be vertew of larges,
His tresory encresis of richess
And sal aganne the mor al-out resave.
For he to quhome he gevith sall have
First his body, syne his hart with two,
His gudis al for to dispone also
In his service; and mor atour he shall
Have o thing, and that is best of all:
That is to say, the worship and the loss
That upone larges in this world furth goss.
And yow shal knaw the lawbour and the press
Into this erth about the gret richess

Is ony bot apone the causs we see
Of met, of cloth, and of prosperitee.
All the remanant stant apone the name
Of purches, furth apone this worldis fame.
And well yow wot, in thyne allegians
Ful many is, the wich haith sufficians
Of everything that longith to ther ned.
What haith yow more, qwich them al to-lede,
For al thi realmys and thi gret riches
If that yow lak of worschip the encress?
Well less al-out, for efter thar estate
Thei have uorschip and kepith it algat;
And yow degradith al thyne hie dugree
That so schuld shyne into nobelitee,
Throuch vys and throw the wrechitness of hart.
And knowis yow not what sall by thi part,
Out of this world when yow sal pass the courss?
Fair well, iwyss; yow never shall recourss
Whar no prince more shall the subjet have
But be als dep into the erd ygrave,
Sauf vertew only and worschip wich abidith
With them, the world apone the laif devidith.
And if he, wich shal eftir the succed,
By larges spend, of quhich that yhow had dreid,
He of the world comendit is and prisit,
And yow stant furth of everything dispisit.

"The puple saith and demyth thus of thee:
'Now is he gone, a verray urech was hee,
And he the wich that is our king and lord
Boith vertew haith and larges in accorde.
Welcum be he!' And so the puple soundith.
Thus through thi viss his vertew mor aboundith,

And his vertew the more thi vice furth schawith.
Wharfor yhe, wich that princes ben yknawith,
Lat not yhour urechit hart so yhow dant
That he that cummyth next yhow may avant
To be mor larg, nore more to be commendit;
Best kepit is the riches well dispendit.
O yhe, the wich that kingis ben, fore sham
Remembrith yhow this world hath bot o naamm
Of good or evill, efter yhe ar gone.
And wysly tharfor chessith yhow the tonn
Wich most accordith to nobilitee
And knytith larges to yhour hie degré.
For qwhar that fredome in o prince ringnis,
It bryngith in the victory of kingis
And makith realmys and puple boith to dout
And subectis of the cuntré al about.
And qwho that thinkith ben o conquerour,
Suppos his largess sumquhat pas mysour,
Ne rak he nat bot frely iffith ay;
And as he wynyth beis uar alway
To mych nor yhit to gredy that he hold,
Wich sal the hartis of the puple colde
And lov and radour cummyth boith two
Of larges. Reid and yhe sal fynd it so.
Alexander, this lord the warld that wan,
First with the suerd of larges he began
And as he wynith ifith largely;
He rakith nothing bot of chevelry
Wharfor of hyme so passith the renown
That many o cetee and many o strang townn
Of his worschip that herith the recorde
Dissirith so to haveing sich o lorde
And offerith them withouten strok of spere,

Suppos that thei war manly men of were,
But only for his gentilless that thei
Have hard. And so he lovit was alway
For his larges, humilitee and manhed
With his awn folk that nevermore, we reid,
For al his weris nor his gret travell,
In al his tym that thei hyme onys faill.
Bot in his worschip al thar besynes
Thei set and levith into no distres.
Wharthrow the suerd of victory he berith.
And many prince full oft the palm werith,
As has ben hard, by largess of before,
In conqueringe of rignis and of glore.
And wrechitnes richt so, in the contrar,
Haith realmys maid ful desolat and bare
And kingis broght doun from ful hie estat,
And who that red ther old bukis wat.
The vicis lef, the vertew have in mynde
And takith larges in his awn kynd,
Amyd standing of the vicis two,
Prodegalitee and averice also.
Wharfor herof it nedith not to more,
So mych therof haith clerkis urit tofore.
Bot who the vertw of larges and the law
Sal chess mot ned considir well and knaw
Into hymeself and thir thre wnderstande:
The substans first, the powar of his land
Whome to he iffith and the causs wharfore,
The nedful tyme awatith evermore.
Kepith thir thre; for qwho that sal exced
His rent, he fallith sodandly in nede.
And so the king that onto myster drowis,
His subjettis and his puple he ovrthrawis

And them dispolyeith boith of lond and rent.
So is the king, so is the puple schent.
Forquhi the voice it scrikth up ful evyne
Without abaid and passith to the hevyne
Whar God Hymeself resavith ther the crye
Of the oppresioune and the teranny
And uith the suerd of vengans doun ysmytith,
The wich that carvith al to sor and bitith
And hyme distroyth, as has ben hard or this
Of every king that wirkith sich o mys.
For ther is few eschapith them; it sall
Boith upone hyme and his successione fall.
For He, forsuth, haith ifyne hyme the wond
To justefy and reull in pece his lond,
The puple all submytit to his cure.
And he agan oneto no creatur
Save only shall unto his Gode obey.
And if he passith so far out of the wey,
Them to oppress, that he shuld reul and gid
Ther heritag, there gwdis to devide,
Ye, wnder whome that he most nedis stond,
At correccioune sal strek his mychty hond,
Not every day, bot shal at onys fall
On hyme, mayhap, and his succescione all.
In this, allace, the blyndis of the kingis
And is the fall of princis and of rygnis.
The most vertew, the gret intellegens,
The blessit tokyne of wysdom and prudens
Iss, in o king, for to restren his honde
Frome his pupleis riches and ther lond.
Mot every king have this vice in mynd
In tyme and not when that he ned fynde.
And in thi larges beith war, I pray,

Of nedful tyme, for than is best alway.
Avyss the ek quhome to that thow salt if,
Of there fam and ek how that thei leif;
And of the vertws and vicious folk also,
I the beseich devidith well thir two
So that thei stond nocht in o degree.
Discreccioune sall mak the diversitee
Wich clepith the moder of al vertewis.
And beith war, I the beseich of this,
That is to say of flatry, wich that longith
To court and al the kingis larges fongith.
The vertuouss man no thing tharof resavith.
The flattereris now so the king dissavith
And blyndith them that wot nothing, iwyss,
When thei do well or quhen thei do omyss,
And latith kingis oft til wnderstonde
Thar vicis and ek the faltis of ther lond.
Into the realme about o king is holde
O flatterere were than is the stormys cold,
Or pestelens, and mor the realme anoyith;
For he the law and puple boith distroyith.
And into principall ben ther three thingis
That caussith flattereris stonding with the kingis:

"And on, it is the blyndit ignorans
Of kingis wich that hath no governans
To wnderstond who doith sich o myss;
But who that farest schewith hym, iwyss,
Most suffisith and best to his plesans.
Wo to the realme that havith sich o chans!

"And secundly, quhar that o king is
Veciuss hymeself, he cherissith, ywys,

Al them the wich that oneto vicis soundith
Wharthrow that vicis and flattery ek aboundith.

"The thrid is the ilk schrewit harrmful vice,
Wich makith o king within hymeself so nyce
That al thar flattry and ther gilt he knowith
Into his wit and yhit he hyme withdrowith
Them to repref and of ther vicis he wot;
And this it is wich that dissemblyng hot
That in no way accordith for o king.
Is he not set abuf apone his ringne
As soverane his puple for to lede?
Whi schuld he spare or quhom of schuld he dred
To say the treuth, as he of right is hold?
And if so ware that al the kingis wold
When that his legis comytit ony vyce
As beith not to schamful nore to nyce
That thei presume that he is negligent
But als far as he thinkith that they mysswent
But dissemblyng reprevith as afferis
And pwnice them quhar pwnysing requeris,
Sauf only mercy in the tyme of ned.
And so o king he schuld his puple led
That no trespass that cummyth in his way
Shuld pass his hond wnepwnist away,
Nor no good deid into the samyn degree,
Nore no vertew suld wnreuardid bee.
Than flattry shuld, that now is he, be low,
And vice from the kingis court withdrow.
His ministeris that shuld the justice reull
Shuld kep well furth of quiet and reull
That now, God wat, as it conservit is,
The stere is lost and al is gon amys.

And vertew shuld hame to the court hyme dress
That exillith goith into the wildernes.
Thus if o king stud lyk his awn degree,
Vertwis and wyss than shuld his puple bee
Only set by vertew hyme to pless
And sore adred his wisdom to displess.
And if that he towart the vicis draw,
His folk sall go on to that ilk law.
What shal hyme pless, thai wil nocht ellis fynd
Bot therapon setith al ther mynde.
Thus only in the vertew of o king
The reull stant of his puple and his ringne,
If he be wyss and, but dissemblyng, schewis,
As I have said, the vicis oneto schrewis.
And so thus, sir, it stant apone thi will
For to omend thi puple or to spill,
Or have thi court of vertewis folk or fullis.
Sen yow art holl maister of the scoullis,
Teichith them and thei sal gladly leir--
That is to say, that thei may no thing heir
Sauf only vertew towart thyn estat.
And cheriss them that vertews ben algait.
And thinkith what that vertew is to thee:
It plessith God, uphaldith thi degree."

"Maister," quod he, "me think rycht profitable
Yowr conseell is and wonder honorable
For me and good. Rycht well I have consavit
And in myne hartis inwartness resavit.
I shall fulfill and do yowr ordynans
Als far of wit as I have suffisans.
Bot Y beseich yow intil hartly wyss
That of my drem yhe so to me devyss,

The wich so long haith occupeid my mynd,
How that I shal no maner sucour fynd
Bot only throw the wattir lyon and syne
The leich that is withouten medysyne;
And of the consell of the flour; wich ayre
Wonderis lyk that no man can duclar."
"Now, sir," quod he, "and I of them al thre
What thei betakyne shal I schaw to the.
Such as the clerkis at them specefiit,
Thei usit nothing what thei signefiit.
The wattir lyone is the God verray.
God to the lyone is lyknyt many way;
But thei have Hyme into the wattir senn;
Confusit were ther wittis al, Y wenn.
The wattir was ther awn fragelitee
And thar trespas and thar inequitee
Into this world, the wich thei stond yclosit;
That was the wattir wich thei have supposit
That haith there knowlag maad so inperfyt.
Thar syne and ek ther worldis gret delyt,
As clowdy wattir was evermore betwenn
That thei the lyone perfitly hath nocht senn,
Bot as the wattir wich was ther awn synne
That evermor thei stond confusit in.
If thei haith stond into religionn clen,
Thei had the lyone not in watter sen
Bot clerly up into the hevyne abuf,
Eternaly whar He shal not remufe.
And evermore in uatter of syne was Hee,
Forquhi it is impossebleze for to bee.
And thus the world, wich that thei ar in
Yclosit is in dyrknes of ther syne;
And ek the thiknes of the air betwen

The lyone mad in uattir to be sen.
For it was nocht bot strenth of ther clergy
Wich thei have here (and it is bot erthly)
That makith them there resouns devyss
And se the lyone thus in erthly wyss.
This is the lyone, God and Goddis Sone,
Jhesu Crist, wich ay in hevyne sal wonne.
For as the lyone of every best is king,
So is He lord and maister of al thing,
That of the Blessit Vyrgyne uas ybore.
Ful many a natur the lyone haith, quharfore
That he to God resemblyt is, bot I
Lyk not mo at this tyme specify.
This is the lyone--tharof have yow no dred--
That shal the help and comfort in thi ned.

"The sentens here now woll I the defyne
Of Hyme, the Lech withouten medysyne,
Wich is the God that everything hath uroght.
For yow may know that uther is it noght
As surgynis and fesicianis, wich that delith
With mortell thingis and mortell thingis helyth
And al thar art is into medysyne,
As it is ordanit be the mycht devyne,
As plasteris, drinkis, and anounytmentis seir,
And of the qualyté watyng of the yher
And of the planetis disposicioune
And of the naturis of compleccyoune,
And in the diverss changing of hwmowris.
Thus wnder reull lyith al there cwris.
And yhit thei far as blynd man in the way,
Oft quhen that deith thar craft list to assay.
Bot God, the wich that is the soveran Lech,

Nedith no maner medysyne to sech;
For ther is no infyrmyté nore wound
Bot as Hyme lykith al is holl and sound.
So can He heill infyrmytee of thoght,
Wich that one erdly medesyne can noght.
And als the saul that to confusioune goith
And haith with hyme and uther parteis boith,
His dedly wound God helyth frome the ground.
Onto his cure no medysyne is found.
This is His mycht that nevermore shall fyne,
This is the Leich withouten medysyne.
And if that yhow at confessioune hath ben
And makith the of al thi synnis clen,
Yow art than holl and this ilk samyn is He
Schall be thi leich in al necessitee.

"Now of the flour Y woll to the discernn.
This is the flour that haith the froyt eternn;
This is the flour, this fadith for no schour;
This is the flour of every flouris floure;
This is the flour of quhom the Froyt uas bornn;
This ws redemyt efter that we war lornn;
This is the flour that ever spryngith new;
This is the flour that changith never hew;
This is the Vyrgyne; this is the blessit flour
That Jhesu bur that is our Salveour,
This flour wnwemmyt of hir virginitee;
This is the flour of our felicitee;
This is the flour to quhom ue shuld exort;
This is the flour not sessith to support
In prayere, consell, and in byssynes
Us catifis ay into our wrechitnes
Onto hir Sone, the quich hir consell herith;

This is the flour that al our gladness sterith,
Throuch whois prayer mony one is savit,
That to the deth eternaly war resavit
Ne war hir hartly suplicatioune;
This is the flour of our salvatioune,
Next hir Sone, the froyt of every flour;
This is the sam that shal be thi succour
If that the lykith hartly reverans
And service yeld oneto hir excellens,
Syne worschip hir with al thi byssyness.
Sche sal thi harm, sche sall thi ned redress.
Sche sal sice consell if oneto the two,
The Lyone and the soverane Lech also,
Yow sall not ned thi dremm for to dispar
Nor yhit no thing that is in thi contrare.
Now," quod the Maister, "yow may well wnderstand
Tueching thi drem as I have born on hande
And planly haith the mater al declarith
That yhow may know of wich yow was disparith.
The Lech, the Lyone, and the flour also,
Yow worschip them, yow serve them evermo
And ples the world as I have said before.
In governans thus stondith al thi glore.
Do as yow list, for al is in thi honde
To tyne thiself, thi honore and thi londe
Or lyk o prince, o conquerour or king
In honore and in worschip for to ringe."
"Now," quod the King, "I fell that the support
Of yhour consell haith don me sich comfort,
Of every raddour my hart is into ess;
To yhour command, God will, Y sal obess.
Bot o thing is yneuch wnto me:
How Galiot makith his avant that he

Shall have the knycht that only by his honde
And manhed was defendour of my londe,
If that shall fall Y pray yhow tellith me,
And quhat he hecht and of quhat lond is hee."

"What that he hecht, yow shall no forther know;
His dedis sall herefterwart hyme schaw.
Bot contrar the he shall be found no way.
No more tharof as now Y will the say."
With that the King haith at his Maistir tone
His leve, oneto his cuntré for to gonne.
And al the ost makith none abyde
To passing home anone thei can provid.
And to Sir Gawane thei haith o lytter maad,
Ful sore ywound, and hyme on with them haade.

The King, as that the story can declar,
Passith to o ceté that was right fair
And clepit Cardole, into Walis was,
For that tyme than it was the nerest place
And thar he sojornyt twenty-four days
In ryall festing, as the auttore says.
So discretly his puple he haith cherit
That he thar hartis holy haith conquerit.
And Sir Gawan, helyt holl and sound
Be fiftene dais he was of every wounde.
Right blyth therof into the court war thei
And so befell the twenty-fourth day
The King to fall into o hevynes
Right ate his table siting at the mess.
And Sir Gawan cummyth hyme before
And saide hyme, "Sir, yhour thoght is al to sore,
Considering the diverss knychtis sere

Ar of wncouth and strang landis here."
The King ansuert, as into matalent,
"Sir, of my thocht or yhit of myne entent
Yhe have the wrang me to repref; forquhy
Thar levith none that shuld me blam, for I
Was thinkand one the worthiest that levyt
That al the worschip into armys prevyt,
And how the thonk of my defens he had
And of the vow that Galiot haith mad.
But I have sen, when that of my houshold
Thar was, and of my falowschip, that wold
If that thei wist, quhat thing shuld me pless,
Thei wald nocht leif for travell nor for ess.
And sumtyme it preswmyt was and said
That in my houshold of al this world I had
The flour of knychthed and of chevalry.
Bot now tharof Y se the contrarye,
Sen that the flour of knychthed is away."
"Schir," quod he, "of resone suth yhe say;
And if God will, in al this warld so round
He sal be soght, if that he may be found."
Than Gawan goith with o knychtly chere;
At the hal dure he saith in this maner:
"In this pasag who lykith for to wend?
It is o jorné most for to comend
That in my tyme into the court fallith,
To knyghtis wich that chevellry lovith
Or travell into armys for to hant.
And lat no knycht fra thynefurth hyme avant
That it denyith." With that onon thei ross,
Al the knychtis, and frome the burdis goss.
The King that sauch, into his hart was wo
And said, "Sair Gawan, nece, why dois yow so?

Knowis yow nocht I myne houshold suld encress
In knychthed and in honore and largess?
And now yow thinkith mak me dissolat
Of knychtis and my houss transulat
To sek o knycht and it was never more
Hard sich o semblé makith o before."
"Sir, quod he, "als few as may yhow pless,
For what I said was nothing for myne ess,
Nor for desir of falouschip, forwhy
To pass alone, but cumpany, think I,
And ilk knycht to pass o sundry way.
The mo thei pass the fewar eschef thay,
Bot thus shal pas no mo bot as yhow lest."
"Takith," quod he, "of quhom yhe lykith best,
Fourty in this pasag for to go."
At this command and Gawan chesit so
Fourty, quhich that he lovit and that was
Richt glaid into his falowschip to pas.
And furth thei go, and al anarmyt thei

Come to the King, withouten more delay,
The relykis brocht, as was the maner tho
When any knyghtis frome the court suld go.
Or when the passit, or quhen thei com, thei swor
The trouth to schaw of every adventur.
Sir Gawan knelyng to his falowis sais,
"Yhe lordis, wich that in this seking gais,
So many noble and worthi knychtis ar yhe,
Methink in vayne yhour travel shuld nocht be;
For adventur is non so gret to pref,
As I suppone, nor yhe sal it esschef.
And, if yhe lyk, as I that shal devyss
Yhour oth to swer, into the samyne wyss,

Myne oith to kep." And that thei undertak,
However so that he his oith mak
It to conserf, and that thei have all swornn.
Than Gawan, wich that was the King beforn,
On kneis swore, "I sal the suth duclar
Of everything when I agan repar
Nor never more aghane sal I returnn
Nore in o place long for to sujornn
Whill that the knycht or verray evydens
I have, that shal be toknis of credens."
His falouschip abasit of that thing
And als therof anoyt was the King,
Saying, "Nece, yow haith al foly uroght
And wilfulness that haith nocht in thi thoght
The day of batell of Galot and me."
Quod Gawan, "Now non other ways ma be."
Tharwith he and his falowschip also
Thar halmys lasit; onto ther horss thei go,
Syne tuk ther lef and frome the court the fare.
Thar names ware to long for to declar.

Now sal we leif hyme and his cumpany
That in thar seking passith bissely;
And of the Lady of Melyhalt we tell,
With whome the knycht mot ned alway duell.

O day she mayd hyme onto hir presens fet
And on o sege besid hir haith hyme set.
"Sir, in keping I have yow halding long,"
And thus sche said, "for gret trespas and wrong,
Magré my stewart, in worschip, and forthi
Yhe suld me thonk." "Madem," quod he, "and I
Thonk yhow so that ever, at my mycht,

Wharso I pass that I sal be yhour knycht."
"Grant mercy, sir, bot o thing I yow pray,
What that yhe ar yhe wold vichsauf to say."
"Madem," quod he, "yhour mercy ask I, quhy
That for to say apone no wyss may I."
"No! Wil yhe not? Non other ways as now
Yhe sal repent, and ek I mak avow
Oneto the thing the wich that I best love,
Out frome my keping sal yhe not remuf
Befor the day of the assemblee,
Wich that, o yher, is nerest for to bee.
And if that yow haith plessit for to say
Yhe had fore me deliverit ben this day;
And I sal knaw, quhether yhe wil or no,
For I furthwith oneto the court sal go
Whar that al thithingis goith and cumyth sonn."
"Madem," quod he, "yhour plesance mot be donne."
With that the knycht oneto his chalmer goith
And the lady hir makith to be wroith
Aganis hyme, but suthly uas sche not,
For he al-out was mor into hir thoght.
Than schapith she agane the ferd day
And richly sche gan hirself aray,
Syne clepit haith apone hir cusynes
And saith, "Y will oneto the court me dress.
And malice I have schawin onto yhon knycht
Forquhy he wold nocht schew me quhat he hicht;
Bot so, iwyss, it is nocht in my thocht,
For worthyar non into this erth is wrocht.
Tharfor I pray and hartly I requer
Yhe mak hyme al the cumpany and chere
And do hyme al the worschip and the ess,
Excep his honore, wich that may hym pless.

And quhen I cum, deliverith hyme als fre
As he is now." "Ne have no dred," quod sche.

The lady partit and hir lef hath ton,
And by hir jorné to the court is gon.
The King hapnit at Logris for to bee,
Wich of his realme was than the chef ceté,
And haith hir met and intil hartly wyss
Resavit her and welcummyt oftsyss
And haith hir home oneto his palice brocht,
Whar that no danté nedith to be socht,
And maid hir cher with al his ful entent.
Eft supir oneto o chalmer ar thei went,
The King and sche and ek the Quen--al thre.
Of hir tithandis at hir than askit hee
And what that hir oneto the court had brocht.
"Sir," quod sche, "I conne not al for nocht;
I have o frend haith o dereyne ydoo,
And I can fynd none able knycht tharto.
For he the wich that in the contrar is
Is hardy, strong and of gret kyne, iwyss.
Bot it is said if I mycht have with me
Your knycht quich in the last assemblé
Was in the feld and the red armys bur,
In his manhed Y mycht my causs assur.
And yhow, sir, richt hartly I exort
Into this ned my myster to support."
"Madem, by faith oneto the Quen I aw,
That I best love, the knycht I never saw
In nerness by which that I hyme knew;
And ek Gawane is gan hyme for to sew
With other fourty knychtis into cumpany."
The lady smylit at ther fantessy.

The Quen tharwith presumyt wel that sche
Knew quhat he was and said, "Madem, if yhe
Knowith of hyme what that he is or quhar,
We yhow besech til ws for to declar."
"Madem," quod sche, "now, be the faith that I
Aw to the King and yhow, as for no why
To court I cam but of hyme to inquere;
And sen of hyme I can no tithingis here,
Nedlyngis tomorn homwart mon I fair."
"Na," quod the King, "madem, ovr son it waire.
Yhe sal remayne her for the Qwenys sak;
Syne shal yhe of our best knychtis tak."
"Sir," quod sche, "I pray yow me excuss,
Forquhy to pass nedis me behuss.
Nor, sen I want the knycht which I have socht,
Wtheris with me to have desir I nocht,
For I of otheris have that may suffice."
Bot yhit the King hir prayt on sich wyss
That sche remanit whill the thrid day,
Syne tuk hir leif to pasing hom hir way.
It nedis not the festing to declar
Maid oneto hir nor company nor fare.
Sche had no knycht, sche had no damyseill
Nor thei richly rewardit war and well.
Now goith the lady homwart and sche
In her entent desyrus is to see
The flour of knychthed and of chevelry:
So was he prysit and hold to every wy.

The lady, which oneto hir palace come,
Bot of schort time remanith haith at home
When sche gart bryng, withouten recidens,
With grete effere this knycht to hir presens

And said hyme, "Sir, so mekil have I socht
And knowith that befor I knew nocht,
That if yhow lyk I wil yhour ransone mak."
"Madem, gladly, wil yhe vichsauf to tak
Efter that as my powar may attenn
Or that I may provid be ony menn."
"Now, sir," sho said, "forsuth it sal be so:
Yhe sal have thre and chess yhow on of tho.
And if yhow lykith them for to refuss
I can no mor, but yhe sal me excuss;
Yhe nedis mot susten yhour adventur
Contynualy inward for til endur."
"Madem," quod he, "and I yhow hartly pray
What that thei say yhe wald vichsauf to say."

"The first," quod sche, "who hath into the chenn
Of lov yhour hart, and if yhe may derenn.
The next, yhour nam, the which ye sal not lye.
The thrid, if ever yhe think of chevalry
So mekil worschip to atten in feild
Apone o day in armys wnder scheld
As that yhe dyd the samyne day when yhe
In red armys was at the assemblee."
"Madem," quod he, "is thar non uther way
Me to redem but only thus to say
Of thingis which that rynyth me to blam,
Me to avant my lady or hir name?
But if that I most schawin furth that one,
What suerté schal I have for to gone
At libertee out of this danger free?"
"Schir, for to dred no myster is," quod shee;
"As I am trew and fathfull woman hold,
Yhe sal go fre quhen one of thir is told."

"Madem, yhour will non uther ways I may,
I mone obey. And to the first Y say,
As to declar the lady of myne hart,
My gost sal rather of my brest astart."
(Wharby the lady fayndit al for nocht
The love quhich long hath ben into her thocht.)
"And of my nam, schortly for to say,
It stondith so that one no wyss I may.
Bot of the thrid, madem, I se that I
Mon say the thing that tuechith velany.
For suth it is I trast, and God before,
In feld that I sal do of armys more
Than ever I did, if I commandit bee.
And now, madem, I have my libertee,
For I have said I never thocht to say."
"Now, sir," quod sche, "whenever yhe wil, ye may;
Bot o thing is, I yhow hartly raquer,
Sen I have hold yhow apone such maner,
Not as my fo, that yhe uald grant me till."
"Madem," quod he, "it sal be as yhe will."
"Now, sir," quod sche, "it is nothing bot yhe
Remann with ws wnto the assemblé,
And everythyng that in yhour myster lyis
I sall gar ordan at yhour awn devyss.
And of the day I shall yow certefy
Of the assemblé yhe sal not pas therby."
"Madem," quod he, "It sal be as yhow list."
"Now sir," quod sche, "and than I hald it best
That yhe remann lyk to the samyne degré
As that yhe war, that non sal wit that yhe
Deliverit war. And into sacret wyss
Thus may yhe be. And now yhe sal devyss
What armys that yhow lykyth I gar mak."

"Madem," quod he, "armys al of blak."
With this, this knycht is to his chalmer gonn.
The lady gan ful prevaly disspone
For al that longith to the knycht in feild.
Al blak his horss, his armour, and his scheld;
That nedful is, al thing sche well previdith.
And in hir keping thus with hir he bidith.
Suppos of love sche takyne hath the charg,
Sche bur it clos. Therof sche uas not larg;
Bot wysly sche abstenit hir dissir,
For ellisquhat, sche knew, he was afyre.
Tharfor hir wit hir worschip haith defendit,
For in this world thar was nan mor commendit,
Boith of discreccioune and of womanhed,
Of governans, of nurtur, and of farhed.
This knycht with hir thus al this whil mon duell,
And furth of Arthur sumthing wil we tell--

That walkyng uas furth into his regiounis
And sojornyt in his ceteis and his townis
As he that had of uisdome sufficyans.
He kepit the lore of Maister Amytans
In ryghtwysnes, in festing and larges,
In cherising cumpany and hamlynes.
For he was bissy and was deligent,
And largly he iffith and dispent
Rewardis, boith oneto the pur and riche
And holdith fest throw al the yher eliche.
In al the warld passing gan his name;
He chargit not bot of encress and famme
And how his puples hartis to empless.
Thar gladnes ay was to his hart most ess.
He rakith not of riches nor tressour

Bot to dispend one worschip and honour.
He ifith riches, he ifith lond and rent,
He cherissyth them with wordis eloquent
So that thei can them utraly propone
In his service thar lyves to dispone,
So gladith themme his homely contynans,
His cherisyng, his wordis of plesans,
His cumpany and ek his mery chere,
His gret rewardis and his iftis sere.
Thus hath the King non uthir besynes
Bot cherising of knychtis and largess
To mak hymeself of honour be commend.
And thus the yher he dryvith to the ende.

BOOK 3

The long dirk pasag of the uinter and the lycht
Of Phebus comprochit with his mycht,
The which, ascending in his altitud,
Avodith Saturnn with his stormys rude.
The soft dew one fra the hevyne doune valis
Apone the erth, one hillis and on valis,
And throw the sobir and the mwst hwmouris
Up nurisit ar the erbis and in the flouris
Natur the erth of many diverss hew
Ovrfret and cled with the tendir new.
The birdis may them hiding in the gravis
Wel frome the halk, that oft ther lyf berevis.
And Scilla hie ascending in the ayre
That every uight may heryng hir declar
Of the sessone the passing lustynes.
This was the tyme that Phebus gan hym dress
Into the Rame and haith his courss bygown
Or that the trewis and the yher uas rown,
Which was yset of Galiot and the King
Of thar assemblé and of thar meting.

Arthur haith a fiftene dais before
Assemblit al his barnag and more
That weryng wnder his subjeccioune
Or lovith hyme or longith to his crown,
And haith his jornay tone, withouten let,
Onto the place the wich that was yset
Whar he hath found befor hyme mony o knycht
That cummyng war with al thar holl mycht
Al enarmyt both with spere and scheld
And ful of lugis plantith haith the feld,
Hyme in the wer for to support and serf
At al ther mycht, his thonk for to disserf.
And Gawan, which was in the seking yhit
Of the gud knycht, of hyme haith got no wit,
Remembrith hyme apone the Kingis day
And to his falowis one this wys can say:
"To yhow is knowin the mater, in what wyss
How that the King hath with his ennemys
A certan day that now comprochit nere,
And oneto ws war hevynes to here
That he uar into perell or into dreid
And we away and he of ws haith neid;
For we but hyme no thing may eschef,
And he but ws in honore well may lef.
For, be he lost, we may nothing withstond
Ourself; our honore we tyne and ek our lond.
Tharfor I red we pas onto the King,
Suppos our oth it hurt into sum thing,
And in the feld with hyme for til endur
Of lyf or deth and tak our adventur."
Tharto thei ar consentit everilkon,
And but dulay the have thar jorney tonne.
When that the King them saw, in his entent

Was of thar com right wonder well content,
For he preswmyt no thing that thei wold
Have cummyne but one furth to ther seking hold.
And thus the King his ost assemblit has
Agane the tyme, againe the day that uas
Ystatut and ordanit for to bee,
And everything hath set in the dogré.
And Galiot, that haith no thing forghet
The termys quhich that he befor had set,
Assemblit has, apone his best maner,
His folk and al his other thingis sere
That to o weryour longith to provid
And is ycome apone the tothir syde.
Whar he befor was one than uas he two,
And al his uthir artilyery also
He dowblith hath, that mervell was to senn.
And by the revere lychtit one the grenn
And stronghar thane ony wallit toune
His ost ybout yclosit in randoune.
Thus war thei cummyne apone ather syd
Befor the tyme, themself for to provid.
Or that the trewis was complet and rwn,
Men mycht have sen one every sid begwn
Many a fair and knychtly juperty
Of lusty men and of yong chevalry
Disyrus into armys for to pruf;
Sum for wynyng, sum causith uas for luf,
Sum into worschip to be exaltate,
Sum causit was of wordis he and hate
That lykit not ydill for to ben--
A hundereth pair at onis one the gren.
Thir lusty folk thus can thar tyme dispend
Whill that the trewis goith to the ende.

The trewis past, the day is cummyne ononne;
One every syd the can them to dispone;
And thai that war most sacret and most dere
To Galiot, at hyme the can enquere,
"Who sal assemble one yhour syd tomornne?
Tonycht the trewis to the end is worne."
He ansuerit, "As yhit oneto this were
I ame avysit I wil none armys bere
Bot if it stond of more necessitee,
Nor to the feld will pas bot for to see
Yhone knycht, the which that berith sich o fame."
Than clepit he the Conquest King be name
And hyme commandit thirti thousand tak
Againe the morne and for the feld hyme mak.
And Gawane haith, apone the tother syde
Consulit his eme he schuld for them provid
And that he schuld none armys to hyme tak
Whill Galiot will for the feld hyme mak.
"I grant," quod he, "wharfor yhe mone dispone
Yhow to the feld with al my folk tomorne
And thinkith in yhour manhed and curage
For to recist yhone fowis gret owtrag."

The nycht is gone; up goith the morow gray,
The brycht sone so cherith al the day.
The knychtis gone to armys than in hast.
One goith the scheildis and the helmys last.
Arthuris ost out ovr the furrde thai ryd.
And thai agane, apone the tother syd,
Assemblit ar apone o lusty greyne,
Into o vaill, whar sone thar mycht be seyne
Of knychtis togedder many o pair
Into the feld assemblyng her and thair,

And stedis which that haith thar master lorne;
The knychtis war done to the erth doune borne.
Sir Esquyris, which was o manly knycht
Into hymeself, and hardy uas and wycht
And intill armys gretly for to pryss,
Yhit he was pure, he previt wel oftsyss;
And that tyme was he of the cumpanee
Of Galiot, bot efterwart was hee
With Arthur. And that day into the feild
He come, al armyt boith with spere and scheld,
With ferss desir, as he that had na dout,
And is assemblit evyne apone a rowt.
His spere is gone; the knycht goith to the erd,
And out onon he pullith haith o swerd.
That day in armys previt he rycht well
His strenth, his manhed: Arthuris folk thai fell.
Than Galys Gwynans, with o manly hart,
Which brother was of Ywane the Bastart,
He cummyne is onone oneto the stour
For conquering in armys of honour
And cownterit with Esquyris hath so
Than horss and man, al four, to erth thai go.
And still o quhill lying at the ground
With that o part of Arthuris folk thei found
Till Gwyans and haith hyme sone reskewit.
Aganis them til Esquyris thei sewyt
Of Galiotis well thirti knychtis and mo.
Gwyans goith done and uthir seven also,
The wich war tone and Esquyris relevit.
Than Ywane the Anterus, aggrevit,
With kynnismen oneto the mellé socht.
The hardy knychtis, that one thar worschip thocht,
Cownterit them in myddis of the scheld

Whar many o knycht was born donn in the feld.
Bot thei wich ware one Galiotis part
So wndertakand nor of so hardy hart
Ne ware thei not as was in the contrare.
Sir Galys Gwyans was resqwyt thare
With his falowis, and Esqwyris don bore.
Thar al the batellis cam, withouten more,
On ather part, and is assemblit so
Whar fyfty thousand war thei and no mo.
In o plane besyd the gret rivere
Thirty thousand one Galiotis half thei uare.
Of Arthuris ten thousand and no mo
Thei ware, and yhit thai contenit them so
And in the feld so manly haith bornn
That of thar fois haith the feld forswornn.
The Conquest King, wich the perell knowith,
Ful manly oneto the feld he drowith.
The lord Sir Gawan, coverit with his scheld,
He ruschit in myddis of the feld
And haith them so into his com assayt
That of his manhed ware thei al affrait.
No langer mycht thei contrar hyme endur
Bot fled and goith oneto discumfiture.
And Galiot, wich haith the discumfit sen,
Fulfillit ful of anger and of ten,
Incontinent he send o new poware,
Wharwith the feldis al ovrcoverit ware
Of armyt stedis both in plait and maill,
With knychtis wich war reddy to assaill.
Sir Gawan, seing al the gret suppris
Of fois cummyng into sich o wys,
Togiddir al his cumpany he drew
And confortable wordis to them schew.

So at the cummyng of thar ennemys
Thei them resauf in so manly wyss
That many one felith deithis wound
And wnder horss lyith sobing one the ground.
This uther cummyth into gret desir,
Fulfillit ful of matelent and ire,
So freschly, with so gret o confluens,
Thar strong assay hath don sich vyolens
And at thar come Arthuris folk so led
That thai war ay abaysit and adred.
Bot Gawan, wich that, by this uorldis fame,
Of manhed and of knychthed bur the name,
Haith previt well be experiens;
For only intil armys his defens
Haith maid his falowis tak sich hardyment
That manfully thei biding one the bent.
Of his manhed war mervell to raherss.
The knychtis throw the scheldis can he perss
That many one thar dethis haith resavit.
None armour frome his mychty hond them savit,
Yhit ay for one ther ennemys wor thre.
Long mycht thei nocht endur in such dugree.
The press, it wos so creuell and so strong
In gret anoy and haith continewit longe
That, magré them, thei nedis most abak,
The way oneto thar lugis for to tak.
Sir Gawan thar sufferith gret myschef
And wonderis in his knychthed can he pref.
His falouschip haith mervell that hym saw;
So haith his fois that of his suerd stud aw.
King Arthur, that al this whill beheld
The danger and the perell of the feld,
Sir Ywan with o falowschip he sende,

Them in that ned to help and to defend,
Qwich fond them into danger and in were
And enterit nere into thar tentis were.
Sir Gawan fechtand was one fut at erde
And no defend but only in his swerde
Aganis them both with spere and scheld.
Of Galowa the knycht goith to the erde.
Thar was the batell furyous and woid
Of armyt knychtis. To the grownde thai yhud.
Sir Ywane, that was a noble knyght,
He schew his strenth, he schew thar his gret mycht,
In al his tyme that never of before
Off armys nore of knychthed did he more.
Sir Gawan thar reskewit he of fors,
Magré his fois, and haith hyme set one horss
That frome the first Conquest King he wann.
Bot Sir Gawan so evill was wondit than
And in the feld supprisit was so sore
That he the werss tharof was evermore.
Thar schew the lord Sir Ywan his curage,
His manhed, and his noble vassolage.
And Gawan, in his doing, wald nocht irk
So al the day enduring to the dyrk
Sal them, magré of thar desyre, constren
On athar half fore to depart in twen.
And when that Gawan of his horss uas tonn,
The blud out of his noiss and mouth is gonn,
And largly so passith every wounde,
In swonyng thore he fell oneto the ground.
Than of the puple petee was to here
The lemytable clamour and the chere,
And of the King the sorow and the care,
That of his necis lyf was in disspare.

"Far well," he sais, "my gladnes and my delyt,
Apone knychthed far well myne appetit,
Fare well of manhed al the gret curage,
Yow flour of armys and of vassolage,
Gif yow be lost." Thus til his tent hyme brocht
With wofull hart and al the surrygenis socht
Wich for to cum was reddy at his neid.
Thai fond the lord was of his lyf in dreid,
For wondit was he and ek wondit so
And in his syd ware brokyne ribys two.
Bot nocht forthi the King thai maid beleif
That at that tyme he shuld the deith eschef.

Off Melyhalt the Ladyis knychtis were
Into the feld and can thir tithingis here,
And home to thar lady ar thai went
Til hir to schewing efter thar entent
In every poynt how that the batell stud
Of Galiot and of his multitud;
And how Gawan hyme in the feld hath bornn,
Throw quhoys swerd so many o knycht uas lornn,
And of the knychtly wonderis that he wrocht;
Syne how that he oneto his tent uas brocht.
The lady hard, that lovit Gawan so
She gan to wep; into hir hart uas wo.
Thir tythyngis oneto Lancelot ar gonn,
Wharof that he was wonder wobygone.
And for the lady hastely he sent,
And sche til hyme, at his command, is went.
He salust hir and said, "Madem, is trew
Thir tithingis I her report of new
Of the assemblé and meting of the ost,
And of Sir Gawan, wich that shuld be lost?

If that be swth, adew the flour of armys!
Now nevermore recoveryt be the harmys.
In hyme was manhed, curtessy, and trouth,
Besy travell in knychthed, ay but sleuth,
Humilyté, gentrice, and cwrag.
In hyme thar was no maner of outrage.
Allace, knycht, allace! What shal yow say?
Yow may complen, yow may bewail the day
As of his deith, and gladschip aucht to ses,
Baith menstrasy and festing at the des;
For of this lond he was the holl comfort
In tyme of ned al knychthed to support.
Allace, madem, and I durst say at yhe
Al yhour behest not kepit haith to me,
Wharof that I was in to full belef
Aganne this day that I schuld have my lef
And nocht as cowart thus schamfully to ly
Excludit into cage frome chevalry,
Whar othir knychtis anarmyt on thar stedis
Hawntis ther yhouthhed into knychtly dedis."
"Sir," quod sche, "I red yhow not displess,
Yhe may in tyme herefter cum at es;
For the thrid day is ordanit and shal be
Of the ostis a new assemblé,
And I have gart ordan al the gere
That longith to your body for to were,
Boith horss and armour in the samyne wyss
Of sable, evyne aftir yhour awn devyss.
And yhe sal her remayne oneto the day;
Syne may yhe pass, fore well yhe knaw the way."
"I will obey, madem, to yhour entent."
With that sche goith and to hir rest is went.
One the morn arly up sche ross

Without delay and to the knycht sche gois
And twk hir lef and said that scho uald fare
Onto the court withouten any mare.
Than knelit he and thankit hir oftsys
That sche so mych hath done hyme of gentriss
And hir byhecht ever, at his myght,
To be hir awn trew and stedfast knycht.
Sche thonkith hyme and syne sche goith her way
Onto the King, withowten more delay,
Whar that in honour with King and Qwen sche sall
Rycht thonkfully resavit be withall.
Eft to Sir Gawan thai hir led, and sche
Ryght gladly hyme desyrit for to see.
And sche hyme fond, and sche was glad tharfore,
All uthirways than was hir told before.
The knycht, the wich into hir keping uas,
Sche had commandit to hir cussynece,
Wich cherist hyme apone hir best manere
And comfort hyme and maid hym rycht gud chere.

The days goith; so passith als the nycht.
The thrid morow, as that the sone uas lycht,
The knycht onon out of his bed aross.
The maden sone oneto his chalmer goss
And sacretly his armour one hyme spent.
He tuk his lef and syne his way he went
Ful prevaly, rycht to the samyne grenn
One the revere, whar he befor had ben,
Evyne as the day the first courss hath maad.
Alone rycht thar he hovit and abaade,
Behalding to the bertes whar the Qwenn
Befor at the assemblé he had senn
Rycht so the sone schewith furth his lycht

And to his armour went is every wycht.
One athir half the justing is bygon
And many o fair and knychtly courss is rown.
The Blak Knycht yhit hovyns on his sted;
Of al thar doing takith he no hed
Bot ay apone the besynes of thocht
In beholding his ey departit nocht.
To quhom the Lady of Melyhalt beheld
And knew hyme by his armour and his scheld,
Qwhat that he was. And thus sche said one hycht,
"Who is he yone? Who may he be, yhone knycht
So still that hovith and sterith not his ren
And seith the knychtis rynyng one the grenn?"
Than al beholdith and in princypale
Sir Gawan beholdith most of all.
Of Melyhalt the Lady to hyme maid
Incontinent, his couche and gart be had
Before o wyndew thore, as he mycht se
The knycht, the ost, and al the assemblé.
He lukith furth and sone the knycht hath sen;
And, but delay, he saith oneto the Qwen,
"Madem, if yhe remembir, so it was
The Red Knycht into the samyne place
That vencust al the first assemblé,
Whar that yone knycht hovis, hovit hee."
"Yha," quod the Qwen, "rycht well remembir I;
Qwhat is the causs at yhe inquere and quhy?"
"Madem, of this larg warld is he
The knycht the wich I most desir to see
His strenth, his manhed, his curag, and his mycht,
Or do in armys that longith to o knycht."

By thus, Arthur, with consell well avysit,

Haith ordanit his batellis and devysit:
The first of them led Ydrus King, and he
O worthy man uas nemmyt for to bee.
The secund led Harvy the Reveyll,
That in this world was knycht that had most feill
For to provid that longith to the were,
One agit knycht and well couth armys bere.

The thrid feld deliverit in the hond
Of Angus, King of Ylys of Scotlande,
Wich cusing was one to King Arthur nere.
One hardy knycht he was, withouten were.
The ferd batell led Ywons the King,
O manly knycht he was into al thing.
And thus devysit ware his batellis sere
In every feld fiftene thousand were.

The fift batell the lord Sir Ywan lede,
Whois manhed was in every cuntré dred.
Sone he was oneto Wryne the Kyng,
Forwart, stout, hardy, wyss, and yhing.
Twenty thousand in his ost thai past,
Wich ordanit was for to assemblé last.

And Galiot apone the tothir syde
Rycht wysly gan his batellis to devid.
The first of them led Malenginys the King,
None hardyar into this erth levyng.
He never more out of his cuntré raid,
Nor he with hyme one hundereth knychtis hade.

The secund the First-Conquest King led,
That for no perell of armys uas adred.

The thrid o king clepit Walydeyne,
He led, and was o manly knycht, but weyne.

The ferd, King Clamedeus has,
Wich that Lord of Far Ylys was.
The fift batell, whar forty thousand were,
King Brandymagus had to led and stere,
O manly knycht and previt well oftsyss,
And in his consell wonder scharp and wyss.
Galiot non armys bur that day,
Nor as o knycht he wald hymeself aray,
But as o servand in o habariowne,
O prekyne hat, and ek o gret trownsciownn
Intil his hond and one o cursour set,
The best that was in ony lond to get.
Endlong the revar men mycht behold and see
Of knychtis weryne mony one assemblé
And the Blak Knycht still he couth abyde
Without removyng, one the river syde,
Bot to the bartes to behold and see
Thar as his hart desyrit most to bee.
And quhen the Lady of Melyhalt haith senn
The knycht so stond, sche said oneto the Qwenn,
"Madem, it is my consell at yhe send
Oneto yone knycht, yourself for to commend,
Beseiching hyme that he wald wndertak
This day to do of armys for your sak."
The Quen ansuerit as that hir lykit nocht,
For othir thing was more into hir thocht:
"For well yhe se the perell, how disjont
The adventur now stondith one the point
Boith of my lord, his honore, and his lond,
And of his men, in danger how thai stond;

Bot yhe and ek thir uthere ladice may,
If that yhow lykith, to the knycht gar say
The mesag. Is none that wil yhow let,
For I tharof sal nocht me entermet."
Onto the Quen scho saith, "Her I,
If so it pless thir uthir ladice by,
Am for to send oneto the knycht content."
And al the ladice can tharto assent,
Beseching hir the mesag to devyss,
As sche that was most prudent and most wyss.
Sche grantit and o madenn haith thai tone,
Discret, apone this mesag for till gone.
And Sir Gawan a sqwyar bad also,
With two speris oneto the knycht to go.
The lady than, withouten more dulay,
Haith chargit hir apone this wyss to say,
"Schaw to the knycht, the ladice everilkone
Ben in the court, excep the Quen allon,
Til hyme them haith recommandit oftsyss,
Beseching hyme of knychthed and gentriss
(Or if it hapyne evermore that he shall
Cum quhar thai may, owther an or all,
In ony thing avail hyme or support,
Or do hyme ony plesans or comfort),
He wold vichsaif for love of them this day
In armys sum manhed to assay.
And say, Sir Gawan hyme the speris sent.
Now go; this is the fek of our entent."
The damysell, sche hath hir palfray tone,
The sqwyar with the speris with hir gonn.
The nerest way thai pass oneto the knycht,
Whar sche repete hir mesag haith ful rycht.
And quhen he hard and planly wnderstude

How that the Quen not in the mesag yude,
He spak no word, bot he was not content.
Bot of Sir Gawan, glaid in his entent,
He askit quhar he was and of his fair.
And thai to hyme the maner can duclair.
Than the sqwyar he prayth that he wold
Pass to the feld, the speris for to hold.
He saw the knychtis semblyng her and thare,
The stedis rynyng with the sadillis bare.
His spuris goith into the stedis syde,
That was ful swyft and lykit not to byd.
And he that was hardy, ferss, and stout,
Furth by o syd assemblyng on a rout
Whar that one hundereth knychtis was and mo.
And with the first has recounterit so
That frome the deth not helpith hym his scheld:
Boith horss and man is lying in the feld.
The spere is gone and al in pecis brak;
And he the trunscyoune in his hand hath tak
That two or thre he haith the sadillis reft
Whill in his hond schortly nothing is left.
Syne, to the squyar, of the feld is gonn.
Fro hyme o spere into his hond haith ton
And to the feld returnyt he agayne.
The first he met, he goith one the plan,
And ek the next, and syne the thrid also.
Nor in his hond, nore in his strak was ho.
His ennemys that ueryng in affray
Befor his strok and makith roum alway.
And in sich wyss ay in the feld he urocht,
Whill that his speris gon uar al to nocht.
Wharof Sir Gawan berith uitnesing
Throw al this world that thar uas non levyng,

In so schort tyme so mych of armys wrocht.
His speris gone, out of the feld he socht
And passit is oneto the revere syde,
Rycht thore as he was wont for to abyde
And so beholdyne in the samyne plann
As to the feld hyme lykit nocht agann.
Sir Gawan saw and saith onto the Quen,
"Madem, yhone knycht disponit not, I weynn,
To help ws more, fore he so is avysit.
As I presume, he thinkith hyme dispisit
Of the mesag that we gart to hyme mak.
Yhowreself yhe have so specialy outtak,
He thinkith evill contempnit for to bee,
Considering how that the necessitee
Most prinspaly to yhowr supporting lyis.
Tharfor my consell is, yhow to devyss
And ek yhowreself in yhowr trespas accuss
And ask hyme mercy and yhour gilt excuss.
For well it oucht o prince or o king
Til honore and til cheriss in al thing
O worthi man that is in knychthed previt.
For throw the body of o man eschevit
Mony o wondir, mony one adventure
That mervell war til any creature.
And als ofttyme is boith hard and sen,
Quhar fourty thousand haith discumfit ben
Uith five thousand and only be o knycht.
For throw his strenth, his uorschip and his mycht,
His falowschip sich comfort of hym tais
That thai ne dreid the danger of thar fays.
And thus, madem, I wot withouten were,
If that yhone knycht this day will persyvere
With his manhed for helping of the King,

We sal have causs to dred into no thing.
Our folk of hyme thai sal sich comfort tak
And so adred thar ennemys sal mak
That sur I am, onys or the nycht,
Of forss yhone folk sal tak one them the flycht.
Wharffor, madem, that yhe have gilt to mend,
My consell is oneto yhon knycht ye send."
"Sir," quod sche, "quhat plessith yhow to do
Yhe may devyss and I consent tharto."
Than was the Lady of Melyhalt content
And to Sir Gawan into contynent
Sche clepit the maid, wich that passit ar,
And he hir bad the mesag thus duclar.
"Say the knycht the Quen hir recommendith
And sal correk in quhat that sche offendith
At his awn will, howso hyme list devyss
And hyme exortith in most humyll wyss,
As ever he will, whar that sche can or may
Or powar haith hir charg be ony way,
And for his worschip and his hie manhede
And for hir luf to helpen in that ned
The Kingis honore, his land fore to preserf,
That he hir thonk forever may deserf."
And four squyaris chargit he also
With thre horss and speris ten to go
Furth to the knycht, hyme prayng for his sak
At his raquest thame in his ned to tak.

The maden furth with the sqwyaris is went
Oneto the knycht and schawith ther entent.
The mesag hard and ek the present senn,
He answerit and askith of the Qwen.
"Sir," quod sche, "sche into yhone bartiis lyis,

Whar that this day yhour dedis sal devyss,
Yhowr manhed, yhour worschip and affere,
How yhe contenn and how yhe armys bere,
The Quen hirself and many o lady to
Sal jugis be and uitnes how yhe do."
Than he, whois hart stant in o new aray,
Saith, "Damyceyll, onto my lady say
However that hir lykith that it bee,
Als far as wit or powar is in me,
I am hir knycht; I sal at hir command
Do at I may, withouten more demand.
And to Sir Gawan, for his gret gentriss,
Me recommend and thonk a thousand syss.
With that, o sper he takith in his hond
And so into his sterapis can he stond,
That to Sir Gawan semyth that the knycht
Encresyng gon o larg fut one hycht.
And to the ladice saith he, and the Qwen,
"Yhon is the knycht that ever I have sen
In al my tyme most knychtly of affere
And in hymeself gon farest armys bere."
The knycht that haith remembrit in his thocht
The Qwenys chargis and how sche hym besocht,
Curag can encresing to his hart.
His curser lap and gan onon to start;
And he the sqwaris haith reqwyrit so
That thai with hyme oneto the feld wald go.
Than goith he one, withowten mor abaid,
And ovr the revar to the feld he raid.
Don goith his spere onone into the rest,
And in he goith withouten mor arest
Tharas he saw most perell and most dred
In al the feld and most of held had ned,

Whar semblyt was the First-Conquest King
With mony o knycht that was in his leding.
The first he met, doune goith boith horss and man;
The sper was holl, and to the next he rann
That helpit hyme his hawbrek nor his scheld,
Bot throuch and throuch haith persit in the feld.
Sir Kay, the wich haith this encontyr sen,
His horss he strekith ovr the larg gren
And Syr Sygramors ek the Desyrand,
With Sir Gresown cummyth at thar honde,
Son of the duk and alsua Sir Ywan
The Bastart, and Sir Brandellis onan,
And Gaherss, wich that brothir was
To Gawan. Thir sex in a rass
Deliverly com prekand ovr the feldis
With speris straucht and coverit with thar scheldis,
Sum for love, sum honor to purchess
And aftir them one hundereth knychtis was,
In samyne will, thar manhed to assay.
On his five falowis clepit than Sir Kay
And saith them, "Siris, thar has yhonder ben
A courss that nevermore farar was sen
Maid be o knycht, and we ar cummyn ilkon
Only ws one worschip to dispone.
And never we in al our dais mycht
Have bet axampil than iffith ws yone knycht
Of well doing. And her I hecht for me
Ner hyme al day, if that I may, to bee
And folow hyme at al mycht I sall,
Bot deth or uthir adventur me fall.
With that, thir sex, al in one assent,
With fresch curag into the feld is went.
The Blak Knychtis spere in pecis gonne,

Frome o sqwyar onne uthir haith he tonne,
And to the feld onone he goith ful rycht.
Thir sex with hyme ay holdith at thar mycht.
And than bygan his wonderis in the feld.
Thar was no helme, no hawbryk, nore no scheld,
Nor yhit no knycht so hardy, ferss nore stout,
No yhit no maner armour mycht hald owt
His strenth, nore was of powar to withstond.
So mych of armys dyde he with his honde
That every wight ferleit of his deid
And al his fois stondith ful of dreid.
So besely he can his tyme dispend
That of the speris wich Sir Gawan send,
Holl of them all thar was not levit onne;
Throw wich but mercy to the deyth is gon
Ful many o knycht and many o weriour
That couth susten ful hardely o stour.
And of his horss supprisit ded ar two,
One of his awn, of Gawanis one also;
And he one fut was fechtand one the gren,
When that Sir Kay haith with his falowis senn.
The sqwyar with his horss than to hym brocht.
Magré his fois, he to his courseir socht
Deliverly, as of o mychty hart,
Without steropis into his sadill start,
That every wycht beholding mervell has
Of his strenth and deliver besynes.
Sir Kay, seing his horss, and how that thai
War cled into Sir Gawanis aray,
Askith at the squyar if he knewith
What that he was, this knycht. And he hym schewith
He wist nothing quhat that he was, nore hee
Befor that day hyme never saw with ee.

Than askith he how and one quhat wyss
On Gawanis horss makith hyme sich service.
The sqwar saith, "Forsuth Y wot no more;
My lord ws bad, I not the causs quharfore."
The Blak Knycht, horsit, to the feld can sew
Als fresch as he was in the morow new.
The sex falowis folowit hyme ilkone
And al in front onto the feld ar gonn.
Rycht freschly one thar ennemys thai foght
And many o fair poynt of armys uroght.

Than hapnyt to King Malangins ost
By Ydras King discumfit was and lost
And fled and to the Conquest King ar gonne;
Thar boith the batellis assemblit into one.
King Malengynis into his hart was wo,
For of hymeself no better knycht mycht go.
Thar forty thousand war thai for fiftene.
Than mycht the feld rycht perellus be sen
Of armyt knychtis gaping one the ground.
Sum deith and sum with mony a grevous wond;
For Arthuris knychtis that manly war and gud,
Suppos that uthir was o multitude,
Resavit tham well at the speris end.
Bot one such wyss thai may not lang defend.
The Blak Knycht saw the danger of the feld
And al his doingis knowith quho beheld
And ek remembrith into his entent
Of the mesag that sche haith to hyme sent.
Than curag, strenth encresing with manhed,
Ful lyk o knycht oneto the feld he raid,
Thinking to do his ladice love to have,
Or than his deth befor hir to resave.

Thar he begynyth in his ferss curag
Of armys, as o lyoune in his rag.
Than mervell was his doing to behold.
Thar was no knycht so strong nor yhit so bold
That in the feld befor his suerd he met
Nor he so hard his strok apone hyme set
That ded or wondit to the erth he socht,
For thar was not bot wonderis that he wrocht.
And magré of his fois everilkone,
Into the feld ofttymys hyme alonn
Throuch and throuch he passith to and fro.
For in the ward it was the maner tho
That non o knycht shuld be the brydill tak
Hyme to orest nore cum behynd his bak
Nor mo than on at onys one o knycht
Shuld strik, for that tyme worschip stud so rycht.
Yhit was the feld rycht perellus and strong
Till Arthuris folk set thai contenyt longe.
Bot in sich wyss this Blak Knycht can conten
That thai, the wich that hath his manhed senn,
Sich hardyment haith takyne in his ded,
Them thocht thai had no maner causs of dred
Als long as he mycht owthir ryd or go,
At every ned he them recomfort so.
Sir Kay haith with his falowis al the day
Folowit hyme al that he can or may,
And wondir well thai have in armys previt
And with thar manhed oft thar folk relevit.
Bot well thai faucht in diverss placis sere,
With multitud ther folk confusit were
That long in sich wyss mycht thai nocht contenn.
Sir Kay, that hath Sir Gawans squyaris sen,
He clepit hyme and haith hyme prayt so

That to Sir Harvy the Revell wil he go
And say to hyme, "Ws think hyme evil avysit,
For her throuch hyme he sufferit be supprisit
The best knycht that ever armys bur;
And if it so befell of adventur,
In his defalt, that he be ded or lamyt,
This warld sal have hyme utraly defamyt.
And her ar of the Round Table also
A falouschip that sall in well and wo
Abid with hyme and furth for to endur
Of lyf or deth, this day, thar adventur.
And if so fal discumfyt at thai bee,
The King may say that wonder evill haith he
Contenit hyme and kepit his honore,
Thus for to tyne of chevalry the flour."
The sqwar hard and furth his way raid;
In termys schort he al his mesag said.
Sir Harvy saith, "Y wytness God that I
Never in my days comytit tratory;
And if I now begyne into myne eld,
In evill tyme fyrst com I to this feld.
Bot, if God will, I sal me son discharg.
Say to Sir Kay I sal not ber the charg;
He sal no mater have me to rapref.
I sal amend this mys if that I lef."
The sqwyar went and tellit to Sir Kay.

And Sir Harvy, in al the hast he may,
Assemblyt hath his ostis and ononn
In gret desyre on to the feld is gon
Befor his folk and haldith furth his way.
Don goith his sper, and evyne before Sir Kay
So hard o knycht he strykith in his ten

That horss and he lay boith apone the gren.
Sir Gawan saw the counter that he maad
And leuch for al the sarues that he had.
That day Sir Harvy prevyt in the feld
Of armys more than longith to his eld;
For he was more than fyfty yher of ag,
Set he was ferss and yong in his curag.
And fro that he assemblyt his bataill
Doune goith the folk of Galotis al haill.
For to withstond thai war of no poware
And yhit of folk ten thousand mo thei uare.

Kyng Walydone, that sauch on such o wyss
His falowis dangerit with thar ennemys,
With al his folk, being fress and new,
Goith to the feld onon, them to resskew.
Thar was the feld rycht perellus aganne;
Of Arthuris folk ful many on uar slan.

Bot Angus, quhich that lykith not to bid
And saw the perell one the tothir sid,
His sted he strok and with his ost is gon
Whar was most ned; and thar the feld has ton.

Kyng Clamedyus makith non abaid,
Bot with his ost oneto the sid he raid.

And Ywons King, that haith his cummyn sen,
Encounterit hyme in myddis of the grenn.
The aucht batellis assemblyt one this wiss;
On ather half the clamore and the cryiss
Was lametable and petws for til her
Of knychtis wich in diverss placis sere

Wondit war and fallyng to and fro;
Yhit Galyotis folk war twenty thousand mo.

The Blak Knycht than onto hymeself he said,
"Remembir the how yhow haith ben araid,
Ay sen the hour that yow was makid knycht,
With love agane quhois powar and whois mycht
Yow haith no strenth; yow may it not endur,
Nor yhit non uthir erthly creatur.
And bot two thingis ar the to amend,
Thi ladice mercy or thi lyvys end.
And well yhow wot that onto hir presens,
Til hir estat nor til hir excellens,
Thi febilness nevermore is able
For to attan, sche is so honorable.
And sen no way yow may so hie extend,
My verray consell is that yow pretend
This dayÄÄsen yow becummyne art hir knycht
Of hir comand and fechtit in hir sycht--
And well yow schaw, sen yow may do no mor,
That of resone sche sal the thank tharfore,
Of every poynt of cowardy yow scham
And intil armys purchess the sum nam."
With that of love into o new desir
His spere he straucht and swift as any vyre
With al his forss the nerest feld he soght,
His ful strenth in armys thar he uroght,
Into the feld rusching to and fro.
Doune goith the man, doune goith the horss also;
Sum throw the scheld is persit to the hart,
Sum throw the hedÄÄhe may it not astart.
His bludy suerd he dreuch, that carvit so
Fro sum the hed and sum the arm in two;

Sum in the feld fellit is in swonn;
Throw sum his suerd goith to the sadill doune.
His fois waren abasit of his dedis,
His mortell strok so gretly for to dred is.
Whar thai hyme saw, within a lytall space
For dreid of ded, thai levyng hyme the place,
That many o strok ful oft he haith forlornn.
The spedy horss away the knycht hath bornn.
Into his wyrking nevermore he sest,
Nor non abaid he makith nor arest.
His falowis so in his knychthed assuryd,
Thai ar recomfort, thar manhed is recoveryt,
And one thar fois ful fersly thai soght.
Thar goith the lyf of many o knycht to nocht.
So was the batell wonderful to tell,
Of knychtis to se the multitud that fell
That pety was til ony knycht to senn
The knychtis lying gaping on the gren.
The Blak Knycht ay continewit so fast
Whill many one discumfit at the last
Are fled and planly of the feld thei pas.
And Galyot haith wondyr, for he was
Of mor powar, and askit at them qwhy
As cowartis thai fled sa schamfully.
Than saith o knycht, sor wondit in the brayne,
"Who lykith, he may retwrn agayne
Frome qwhens we come, mervalis for to see
That in his tyme never sich sauch hee."
"Marvell," quod he, "that dar I boldly say
Thay may be callit and quhat thai ar, I pray."
"Schir, in the feld forsuth thar is o knycht
That only throw his body and his mycht
Vencussith all that thar may non susten

His strokis, thai ar so fureows and ken.
He farith as o lyone or o beyre,
Wod in his rag, for sich is his affere.
Nor he the knycht into the armys red
Wich at the first assemblé in this sted
Vencussith all and had the holl renown,
He may to this be no comparysoune;
Fore never he sesith sen the day uas gonn
Bot evermore continewit into one."
Quod Galiot, "In nome of God and we
Al, be tyme, the suthfastness sal see."

Than he in armys that he had is gon
And to the feld with hyme agane hath ton
Al the flearis and found yne sich aray
His folk that ner discumfyt al war thay.
Bot quhen thai saw cummyne ovr the plan
Thar lord, thai tuk sich hardement agann
That thar essenyeis lowd thai gon to cry.
He chargit tham to go, that ware hyme by,
Straucht to the feld with al thar holl forss;
And thai, the wich that sparit not the horss,
All redy war to fillyng his command
And freschly went withowten more demand.
Throw qwich thar folk recoveryt haith thar place,
For al the feld preswmyt that thar was
O new ost, one such o wyss thai soght,
Whar Arthuris folk had passith al to nocht.
Ne war that thai the better war ilkonne
And at thai can them utraly disponne
Rathar to dee than flee, in thar entent,
And of the Blak Knycht haith sich hardyment,
For at al perell, al harmys and myschef,

In tyme of ned he can tham al ralef.

Thar was the batell dangerus and strong;
Gret was the pres, bath perellus and throng.
The Blak Knycht is born onto the ground;
His horss hyme falyth, that fellith dethis wound.
The six falowis that falowit hyme al day,
Sich was the press that to the erth go thay.
And thar in myd among his ennemys
He was about enclosit one sich wyss
That quhare he was non of his falowis knew
Nor mycht nocht cum to help hyme nore reskew.
And thus among his ennemys allon
His nakid suerd out of his hond haith ton;
And thar he previt his vertew and his strenth,
For thar was none within the suerdis lenth
That came bot he goith to confusioune.
Thar was no helme, thar was no habirioune
That may resist his suerd, he smytith so.
One every syd he helpith to and fro
That al about the compas thai mycht ken
The ded horss lyith uirslyng with the men.
Thai hyme assalyeing both with scheld and spere:
And he agane, as at the stok the bere
Snybbith the hardy houndis that ar ken,
So farith he; for never mycht be sen
His suerd to rest that in the gret rout
He rowmyth all the compas hyme about.

And Galiot, beholding his manhed,
Within hisself wonderith of his ded
How that the body only of o knycht
Haith sich o strenth, haith sich affere and mycht.

Than said he thus, "I wald not that throw me
Or for my causs that such o knycht suld dee,
To conquer all this world that is so larg."
His horss than can he with his spuris charg
A gret trunsioune into his hond hath ton
And in the thikest of the press is gonn
And al his folk chargit he to sess.
At his command thai levyng al the press;
And quhen he had departit all the rout
He said, "Sir knycht, havith now no dout."
Wich answerit, "I have no causs to dred."
"Yis," quod he, "sa ever God me sped,
Bot apone fut quhill ye ar fechtand here
And yhow defendith apone sich manere
So hardely and ek so lyk o knycht
I sal myself with al my holl mycht
Be yhour defens and uarand fra al harmys.
Bot had yhe left of worschip intil armys,
What I have don I wold apone no wyss.
Bot sen yhe ar of knychthed so to prys
Yhe salt no maner causs have for to dred.
And set yhour horss be falit at this ned,
Displess yhow not, forquhy ye sal not want
Als many as yhow lykith for to hawnt.
And I myself, I sal yhowr sqwyar bee,
And, if God will, never more sal wee
Depart." With that anon he can to lycht
Doune frome his horss and gaf hyme to the knycht.
The lord he thonkit and the horss hath ton,
And als so fresch oneto the feld is gon
As at no strokis he that day had ben.
His falowis glad one horss that hath hym sen,
To Galiot one uthir horss thai broght;

And he goith one and frome the feld he socht
And to the plan quhar that his ostis were.
And Brandymagus chargit he to stere
Efter hyme within a lytill space,
And ten thousand he takyne with hym hass.
Towart the feld onon he can to rid
And chargit them befor the ost to byd.
Wp goith the trumpetis and the claryownis,
Hornys, bugillis blawing furth thar sownis,
That al the cuntré resownit hath about.
Than Arthuris folk uar in dispar and dout
That hard the noys and saw the multitud
Of fresch folk: thai cam as thai war wod.

Bot he that was withowten any dred,
In sabill cled, and saw the gret ned
Assemblyt al his falowis and arayd.
And thus to them in manly termes said:
"What that ye ar I knaw not yhour estat;
Bot of manhed and worschip, well I wat,
Out throuch this warld yhe aw to be commendit,
This day ye have so knychtly yhow defendit.
And now yhe see how that, aganis the nycht,
Yhour ennemys pretendit, with thar myght
Of multitud and with thar new ost
And with thar buglis and thar wyndis bost
Freschly cummyng into sich aray,
To ifyne yhow one owtray or affray.
And now almost cummyne is the nycht,
Quharfor yhour strenth, yhour curag and yhour
    mycht
Yhe occupye into so manly wyss
That the worschip of knychthed and empryss

That yhe have wonyng and the gret renown
Be not ylost, be not ylaid doune.
For one hour the sufferyng of distress,
Gret harm it war yhe tyne the hie encress
Of uorschip servit al this day before.
And to yhow al my consell is, tharfore,
With manly curag but radour yhe pretend
To met tham scharply at the speris end
So that thei feil the cold speris poynt
Outthrow thar scheldis in thar hartis poynt
So sal thai fynd we ar nothing affrayt,
Wharthrouch we sall the well less be assayt.
If that we met them scharply in the berd,
The formest sal mak al the laif afferd."
And with o voyss thai cry al, "Sir knycht
Apone yhour manhed and yhour gret mycht
We sal abid for no man shall eschef
Frome yhow this day, his manhed for to pref."
And to his ost the lord Sir Ywane said,
"Yhe comfort yow, yhe be nothing affrayd.
Ws ned no more to dreding of suppriss:
We se the strenth of al our ennemys."
Thus he said, for he wend thai uar no mo,
Bot Sir Gawan knew well it uas not so;
For al the ostis mycht he se al day
And the gret host he saw quhar that it lay.
And Galiot, he can his folk exort,
Beseching them to be of good comfort
And sich enconter ...

[The MS ends at this point. Lines 299-313 indicate the general content of the entire romance and thus give some indication of how it would have concluded.]

MORE ARTHURIAN LEGENDS

We'd love for you to join our community! For more Arthurian texts, resources, and fiction, visit some of the links below!

The Website
www.arthurlegends.com
www.mythbank.com

Facebook
www.facebook.com/arthurianlegendsuniverse

Instagram
instagram.com/arthurian_legends

Printed by Amazon Italia Logistica S.r.l.
Torrazza Piemonte (TO), Italy

12397756R00069